DESCENT

Praise for Julie Cannon

In *Power Play*, "Cannon gives her readers a high stakes game full of passion, humor, and incredible sex."—*Just About Write*

"*Heart 2 Heart* has many hot, intense sex scenes; Lane and Kyle sizzle across the pages…Cannon has given her readers a read that's fun as well as meaty."—*Just About Write*

In *Heartland* "[t]here's nothing coy about the passion of these unalike dykes—it ignites at first encounter, and never abates…Cannon's well-constructed novel conveys more complexity of character and less overwrought melodrama than most stories in the crowded genre of lesbian-love-against-all-odds—a definite plus."—*Book Marks*

In *Heartland*, "Julie Cannon has created a wonderful romance. Rachel and Shivley are believable, likeable, bright, and funny. The scenery of the ranch is beautifully described, down to the smells, work, and dust. This is an extremely engaging book, full of humor, drama, and some very hot, hot sex!"—*Just About Write*

"Cannon has given her readers a novel rich in plot and rich in character development. Her vivid scenes touch our imaginations as her hot sex scenes touch us in many other areas. *Uncharted Passage* is a great read."—*Just About Write*

"Julie Cannon's novels just keep getting better and better! [*Just Business*] is a delightful tale that completely engages the reader. It's a must read romance!"—*Just About Write*

Visit us at www.boldstrokesbooks.com

By the Author

Come and Get Me

Heart 2 Heart

Heartland

Uncharted Passage

Just Business

Power Play

Descent

DESCENT

by
Julie Cannon

2010

DESCENT
© 2010 BY JULIE CANNON. ALL RIGHTS RESERVED.

ISBN 10: 1-60282-160-7
ISBN 13: 978-1-60282-160-6

THIS TRADE PAPERBACK ORIGINAL IS PUBLISHED BY
BOLD STROKES BOOKS, INC.
P.O. BOX 249
VALLEY FALLS, NY 12185

FIRST EDITION: AUGUST 2010

CREDITS
EDITOR: CINDY CRESAP
PRODUCTION DESIGN: STACIA SEAMAN
COVER DESIGN BY SHERI (GRAPHICARTIST2020@HOTMAIL.COM)

Acknowledgments

Thank you never seems to be enough to say to all the people behind the scenes who allow my fantasies to come to life on the page. Unfortunately, that's all I have, and because they are who they are, that's all they need. Thanks.

Dedication

For Laura
Every single one, every single time.

PROLOGUE

*D*on't fall, don't stumble, don't trip, the cadence in her head echoed with each step. Her head was spinning, her heart racing in direct competition with her shaking legs as she climbed to the top of the winner's platform. The crowd chanted her name as she finally arrived at her destination.

This was more than about winning. Much, much more. It was the achievement of everything she had worked a lifetime for. Millions of beads of sweat, thousands of hours of practice, and untold sacrifices to get to this point. She was the best in the world. She had proven it. To herself, her critics, and her adversaries.

She was finally here. She should be euphoric, ecstatic, on top of the world. This should be the happiest day of her life. But all she felt was empty. Hundreds of people surrounded her, but she was alone, totally alone when it really mattered.

She scanned the crowd searching for the only person that mattered. She recognized many familiar faces, but none contained the crystal clear eyes that she desperately wanted to see.

Her name was called and she stepped forward.

CHAPTER ONE

"Yeah, baby," Shannon shouted into the cool, crisp morning air. The sun was at her back and the dew on the pine trees to her right had evaporated under the warm rays of the first day of June. Gripping her handlebars tightly and bending her knees, she pulled her lithe body and ultra-light carbon frame bike up and over the root snaking diagonally across the trail. Her thighs worked in tandem with the shocks on the front and rear of her custom-made bicycle and she landed on the hard dirt path with barely an impact.

She dodged a low-hanging branch and flew down the mountain, zigzagging around rocks, downed trees, and an occasional squirrel scampering across her path. The trail was a single track, no wider than one rider could traverse, one of her favorites. The trail was bound on one side by rocks and trees while the other dangerously dropped off the side of the mountain. She was in the middle of the San Bernardino Forest in central California careening down Big Bear Mountain and life didn't get much better than this.

At the base of the trail she skidded to a stop, turned around, and looked at the path she just descended. She pumped her fist into the air. "Gotcha this morning, girl. This time I beat you. It's about time." She faced the eight-thousand-foot mountain behind her. "I don't need another patch of road rash or bent frame." She took a long drink from her CamelBak, the water inside still cool.

Her monologue with the mountain complete, Shannon pedaled across the dirt parking lot to the chair lift that would take her back to the top of the mountain. It would be her fourth ride of the day and she would push herself harder this time. The championship series was less than a month away. Eleven races over thirteen weeks in Canada and several countries in Europe including Andorra, Spain, and Switzerland, culminating with the twenty-four-hour mountain bike championship in Australia that would determine the world's best rider.

This time Shannon had to wait in line to board the Snow Summit Scenic Sky Chair. It was after ten and the tourists had arrived to ride the breathtaking Sky Chair to the top of Big Bear Mountain. Once at the summit everyone from walkers, recreational bikers, pro riders, and everything in between would find a trail to suit their skill level. If nothing else, they could have a light snack at the restaurant and eat on picnic tables overlooking the dark blue of Big Bear Lake.

Shannon's critical eye told her that the couple sliding onto the lift chair were going to neck the entire eighteen-minute ride, the elderly man behind them would head directly for one of the hiking trails, and she hoped the baby boomers in front of her stayed on the gentle North Shore bike path.

She stepped forward watching the lift operator assist riders onto the chair or hang their bikes on the hooks specially made for the summer riders. The woman had been working the lift on her earlier rides and Shannon had made good use of the time in line. The worker was cute in a baby butch kind of way with a rock-hard ass, well-defined muscles in her legs, and an equally impressive physique from the waist up. She looked vaguely familiar but Shannon couldn't put her finger on where she had seen her before. She hoped she hadn't *been with* her and didn't remember.

Jackie was stamped into the name tag pinned high on the prominent breasts and when she caught and held Shannon's eye they conveyed equal interest.

"Going up again?" Jackie asked none too subtly as her gaze ran up and down Shannon's body. Her tight bike shorts and tank top left little if anything to the imagination, but the look on Jackie's face said her imagination was working just fine. She reached for Shannon's bike to hang it on the hook.

Shannon held firm to her bike and Jackie's gaze once it finally stopped on her face. Her pulse sped up, her stomach tingled in that familiar way it did when she was attracted to someone, and she sensed a liaison on the horizon. Out of the peripheral of her vision, Shannon noticed that the handlebar of her bike was just low enough to be in direct line with Jackie's crotch. Keeping eye contact, she edged the bike closer and when Jackie's eyes widened and grew dark, Shannon knew she hit her mark.

"Actually, I prefer going down. The faster the better." She arched an eyebrow as if to say, "I know you know what I mean."

Three chairs arrived and left the entry point before Jackie responded. Her voice was low and suggestive.

"I didn't doubt it for a minute." She looked around as if checking for her boss or anyone within earshot. "Speaking of minutes, I have a break in fifteen." She nodded in the direction of the top of the lift.

Why not, Shannon thought. It had been a few weeks since she had enjoyed the company of another woman and this one was certainly willing. It was obvious she wasn't looking for love. At least Shannon hoped she wasn't. It might be awkward afterward with Jackie working at the lift, but it wouldn't be the first time she ran into a previous lover. She knew what to do. She had plenty of experience in how to handle that situation.

"About a quarter mile east on 210N are two downed trees," Shannon replied referring to one of the trails identified by the markers along the path. She was rewarded with a sly wink and a look that promised much more than what she had come to the mountain for.

Chapter Two

How many times are you going to lift that?"
"Just one more set."

"Caroline, you've already done at least five and that's only the ones I saw. Who knows how many I didn't. We've been here for two hours. You're going to hurt yourself."

Gritting her teeth, Caroline lifted the weight bar over her chest. She was on her back, her arms shaking, and she felt her left arm begin to lose strength. The bar started to shift dangerously.

"God damn it, Caroline," her best friend Fran Loming growled as she stepped forward to take the weight out of her hands and put it back in the bracket. "Now you're being stupid."

"Okay, okay, you win," Caroline said, sitting up.

"It's not about me winning. It's about you. You're pushing yourself too hard."

Caroline wiped the sweat from her face, giving herself a few extra seconds before she had to respond. Fran was only three days older than Caroline and was equally dedicated to her thrice weekly workout. They met their freshman year at Columbia, and after a few short months exchanged roommates and lived together for the remainder of their undergrad years and their advanced degree as well.

"I know, I know," Caroline replied with absolutely no intention of letting up on her training regime. If anything, she was going to step it up a notch.

"Why is it I don't believe you?"

Caroline didn't have to see the look on Fran's face to know she was probably rolling her eyes at her. "Because I'm committed to winning this year?" she asked over her shoulder as she approached the stationary bikes. She knew Fran would follow her.

"And why is this year any different? Do you expect me to believe that for the past ten years you've been screaming down mountains, negotiating hairpin turns, peeling more than an acre or two of skin off your bones, and almost killing yourself, more than once I might add, just for something to do on the weekend? And why in the hell are you getting on the bike?" Fran pointed at the stationary machine. "Doesn't your ass spend enough time in the saddle?"

Caroline could only shake her head. "Fran, it's not that bad. I haven't had a serious fall since the one in Arizona and that one wasn't my fault. That bitch Martin cut into my lane." Caroline stifled an involuntary shudder remembering the nasty thirty-foot spill she took down the side of the mountain. More than her pride had been wounded. She had broken her leg in three places and it had taken over twenty stitches to close the gash in her left arm. She was very lucky. If a large boulder had not stopped her fall, it would have been much worse.

"I don't care whose fault it was, and that's beside the point."

Caroline loved Fran, and at one time hoped there might be something more between them than just friends, but Fran was as straight as they came and Caroline didn't want to lose her as a friend. They had seen each other through numerous boyfriends, girlfriends, jobs, cars, and races. Fran was a recreational mountain bike rider, more interested in seeing nature than conquering it.

Fran looked at her with the exasperated expression that was, unfortunately, far too familiar to Caroline. "Come on, Fran, you know how much this championship means to me." Fran did, and Caroline didn't know why she asked such a stupid question. She had been training practically nonstop for the past twelve months, determined to be in top physical condition going into the world mountain bike championships. The last five months she'd ridden in several smaller races to get her body back into the groove of biking again.

The championship was run on some of the toughest downhill courses in the world. The scoring was similar to the Tour de France where riders earned points from not only winning a specific race but also based on their race time and if they finished in the top three places. Every race was a different distance, technically more complex as the series continued, and grueling as they passed through several different time zones every two weeks.

"I know, I know, knucklehead. I want you to win almost more than you do. I'm tired of traipsing all over the world after you." Fran's attention was drawn to a buff thirtysomething walking by with more than a few hard muscles.

Caroline took advantage of her distraction to increase her pace for a quick sprint. Before she had a chance to finish, Fran was turning back to her. She slowed down, too tired to spar with her. Fran was an attorney and Caroline lost every argument. She climbed off the bike and took a swig of the blue liquid in her water bottle. "You love it and you know it. What was his name, Carlos or something or another? You know, the one in São Paulo? Or was it Belize?" Caroline snapped her fingers. "No, I remember it was—" She didn't get a chance to finish before Fran swatted her with her towel.

"Shut up. It was Julian in São Paulo and Gerhard in Amsterdam." They walked into the locker room shedding their sweat-soaked T-shirts. "You're just jealous," Fran said proudly. "Because I'm getting some and you're too busy training to have someone's hands on your butt instead of a bike seat."

Caroline opened her mouth to rebut her comment but closed it when she realized it was true. When was the last time someone had their hand on her ass? When was the last time she *wanted* someone's hand on her ass, or any other part for that matter?

Caroline wasn't a virgin, but she wasn't getting anywhere near the action Fran was. When she wasn't training, she was studying for her Ph.D. in astrophysics. Other than Fran, she had a few friends but most had given up on her ever going out with them. A wet shirt landed on her head drawing her attention back to the conversation.

"Hey, CD, you with me?" Fran asked using the nickname she insisted on calling Caroline after watching her race for the first time. Caroline was too hard a name to scream in encouragement, and her last name of Davis was too butch, so Fran settled on Caroline's initials instead.

"Yeah, I'm here." Caroline tossed the stinky garment back at her. Suddenly feeling like she owed Fran more than simple thanks for sticking with her, she stripped down to her birthday suit and dashed toward the showers. "Last one out of the shower buys the drinks at Maloney's." She heard Fran shriek as she shut the curtain behind her.

❖

Fran was on her second Cape Cod when Caroline finished her third bottle of water. She was never much of a drinker and certainly not two weeks before the first race of the series. Maloney's was the only lesbian bar in Stockton, a little more than a wide spot in the road fifty miles due west of Colorado Springs. Caroline had been training there for the past six months getting acclimated to the high altitude as well as honing her skill on the dozens of downhill courses in the area.

Caroline glanced around the room. It was a typical bar with two pool tables in a room to the right and high tables scattered around a square dance floor where she had scooted her boots with a few local girls. Even though she was in training, Caroline wasn't dead and one of the first things she noticed when she moved to Stockton was that more than just the countryside was breathtaking.

"Go talk to her."

Fran nudged Caroline in the side. "What?"

"Go talk to her." Fran nodded toward a woman sitting at the end of the bar.

"Who?"

"Who, hell, Caroline. The woman over there you can't stop looking at." Fran lifted her head and nodded in the direction of the woman sitting three tables away. She had long blond hair, and what drew Caroline's attention were the firm, tanned limbs jetting out from cutoff jeans and a yellow tank top. God, she loved summer in the Rockies.

"Go on." Fran nudged her.

"I'm not leaving you here. *We* came to have a drink, not for *me* to pick up a woman." Caroline took another sip of her water. The woman was striking, Caroline thought as she glanced over quickly. "And for God's sake, Fran," Caroline looked at her watch, "it's three in the afternoon."

"You're here, she's here, who gives a shit what time it is? I'd dump you in a heartbeat if I had someone like that looking at me like I was dessert."

"What are you talking about?" Caroline looked up as the bartender placed another bottle of water in front of her.

"You know what I mean. I've dumped you on more than one occasion in just this situation when some guy caught my fancy. And she's looking at you as much as you are looking at her and you both know it. I'm a big girl. I can find my way home. Now go."

Fran elbowed her off the stool. Caroline had a decision to make. She could either go over and introduce herself or be harassed by Fran for weeks about this missed opportunity. The last thing she wanted was the latter and she wasn't sure she was up to the former. It had been a long time since she had started a conversation with a total stranger and even longer since she had been touched by one. Fran was right; she did need a time-out from the nonstop training schedule she had been on. Maybe a little R&R would give her the break she needed before the long trek of events began. Once the first race began, it would be nothing but pressure and competition for the next twelve weeks. The woman looked her way, and even though Caroline was out of practice, there was no mistaking the look of invitation in the woman's eyes. Caroline didn't need to be asked twice.

❖

"Shit," Shannon exclaimed into the neck of the woman in front of her. It was her favorite word when she couldn't think of anything else, and the way her orgasm had just rocketed from the tip of her toes through the top of her head, there was nothing else she could think of. Jackie was every bit as adventurous as Shannon had hoped she would be.

A few minutes earlier when Jackie rounded the corner of the trail, Shannon stepped out from behind a wide pine tree and without saying a word they both disappeared into the thick forest. They had only gone about thirty yards when Shannon was grabbed from behind and pushed up against a large boulder. In an instant one hand was under her shirt, the other inside her bike shorts, and warm, wet lips were on her neck.

She was more than ready, having thought about taking the ride operator out here in the open, under the bright sunshine. Outdoor sex was her favorite and the anticipation had her primed. Jackie had an exquisite mouth and talented fingers. She licked, sucked, and fondled Shannon until she exploded and fell limp, squeezed between Jackie and the hard rock. She let herself be taken away a second time and a third before stilling Jackie's hand with her own. Between the high altitude and the blazing orgasms, Shannon's head spun. She gave herself a few moments to enjoy the sensation then, catching up quickly, had Jackie's shirt over her head and her shorts down around her knees in seconds.

She reversed their positions pinning Jackie to the smooth face of the rock. She didn't waste any time on kissing her, but went straight for the luscious breasts that had tormented her thoughts during the eighteen-minute ride to the top of the mountain. She licked and sucked her way around one large breast, then the other without touching the erect nipples. Jackie grabbed her hair and pulled her closer.

Shannon concentrated on evading the tempting peak and slid down her body planting hard kisses and quick nips on the exposed flesh. She was tempted to linger and tease Jackie's clitoris, but when she realized that her entire pubis area was fully exposed, she could not stop the overwhelming desire to bury her tongue in the pale flesh.

Jackie willingly spread her legs allowing Shannon the access she wanted. She opened her eyes and looked up. Jackie's hands were on her own breasts, her head thrown back as if worshiping the sun riding high in the cloudless sky. Shannon's own desire sparked again as she devoured the scent and taste of Jackie. In a matter of minutes, Jackie grabbed the back of her head and shuddered against her mouth. Shannon tasted the orgasm and with her own trembling hand brought herself to climax again.

CHAPTER THREE

Caroline woke in her own bed with only a vague recollection how she got there. It was still dark and she sat up to see the clock. "Three a.m.? Oh God." She flopped back on the hard mattress. Her mouth tasted like tissue paper, and when she climbed out of bed, the muscles in her normally flexible legs talked back to her.

Paula? Paulette? Pauline? Caroline struggled for the name of the woman who, over the course of more hours than she could remember, had fucked her senseless. She stepped over her dog Max and stumbled into the bathroom. She didn't know what she needed more, to pee or take two aspirin. Necessity and Mother Nature forced the former and she tried to push the aching muscles to the back of her mind.

She had started riding as a way to lose weight when she was in her early teens and had fallen in love with the freedom she felt careening down the mountainside. She missed the early days of riding simply for the sheer joy of it. Exploring bike paths, making her own trails in the deserts of Phoenix, the mountains of Moab or Monument Valley. Every ride was an adventure, an investigation of the terrain, the challenge to her body. And it was her body that reminded her that she had been taken on a very different physical adventure yesterday afternoon.

Paulie, yes, that was it. Paulie had quickly agreed to a game of pool, a drink, another drink, and an early dinner. Caroline was dessert. Or was it Paulie that was dessert? She certainly was a tasty treat even without the whipped cream she offered to pull out of the fridge. They had spent the remaining hours after dinner and before midnight doing almost everything imaginable to each other. At least Caroline thought it was everything. She knew what went where and why, but Paulie had surprised her a few times. She would have to remember those moves for future reference. Not with Paulie of course; that was definitely a one-time thing. But she would keep that technique and new skill in the back of her mind for when the right opportunity came up.

She dropped back into bed for the few more hours of sleep she needed and when her alarm went off at six, she cussed at it. She shuffled into the shower and under the hard, hot spray. She racked her mind to remember what she had to do that day. Riding was a given but there was something she needed too. Note cards! That was it. Her supply of note cards was getting dangerously low and she would have to stop off at OfficeMax on the way to the library.

Caroline was in the final stages of preparing to defend her dissertation on supernova-driven interstellar turbulence and she found that by outlining her main research points on large index cards, she could better organize her thoughts. She knew the data like she knew every bend and dip on her favorite downhill trail, but she was nervous. This was the big time. Her future would be set when she received her Ph.D. in astrophysics. She was going to work for NASA. It was a dream she had since the first time she looked into the sky with the cheap telescope her father bought her for Christmas. Now, after almost twenty years of school, the last seven at Columbia University, everything she had ever worked for was within her grasp.

She was scheduled to stand before a committee of the faculty only three weeks after the final race in the championship series. The actual date she had been given was out of her control. The committee had determined the date and she could either accept or decline. By declining, she would have to reapply and if accepted wait an additional year before the committee met again. Her hands were tied and she had to make the best of it. It would be difficult to concentrate on both her thesis and her races, but Caroline was bound and determined to finish both of these chapters in her life at the top.

❖

Shannon ripped open the envelope with the familiar return address of Mount Holyfield Academy embossed in the thick white paper. MHA, as the students called it, was one of the most prestigious girls' boarding schools in Connecticut. Acceptance was limited to two hundred each year and it had been widely rumored that the daughters of several presidents had been denied admission. Shannon knew how she had received one of the coveted slots, but hadn't really thought about her school years in, well, years.

Christian and Virginia Roberts were the richest of the rich in Palm Beach. Christian was lucky enough to be born into wealth while his wife was skilled enough to marry into it. Shannon was their only child and they provided her with everything. Every earthly thing money could buy, that is. Everything except love.

Her parents didn't know how to love unconditionally. They had not grown up in warm, loving households, but had been raised by a series of nannies and governesses. Her mother had gone to MHA and it was without question her daughter would as well.

Shannon rebelled against the confinement money placed on her. She hated the parties, events, and vacations she had been forced to attend that bored the ever-living hell out of her. The clothes her mother wore were starched within an inch of their life. The dresses were made of only the finest fabric, and her shoes the latest style direct from the runways in Paris. Elizabeth had dressed Shannon in her image the first four years of her life, but it was on her fifth birthday when Shannon strode into the room in a pair of the most expensive pants she had cut off at the knees. She remembered the look on her mother's face and wasn't sure if it was shock for what her child had done or the embarrassment her child caused. Either way, Shannon ceased to be the apple of her mother's eye.

A crisp invitation detailing her ten-year reunion gave Shannon a paper cut. While she sucked the small slit in her finger, she read the information that invited her to dine, reminisce, and reconnect with her fellow alumni. And cough up money, she thought to herself. At least three times a year MHA tracked her down and attempted to guilt her into contributing money to the school. Her parents had doled out enough of their cash while she was there, and Shannon saw no reason why she should after she left. Her education there was done. She had no intention of attending the two-day event.

The invitation and the rest of her mail still in her hand, Shannon detoured into the spare bedroom she had converted to an office. She'd bought the cabin four years ago and it was pretty much in the same condition as when she unlocked the door after getting the keys. It was small by Big Bear Lake standards. The house itself was only two thousand square feet, sitting in the middle of half an acre of prime lakefront property. She hadn't done anything to the interior other than hang a picture here and there. The solid wood floors were covered in throw rugs that she had literally thrown on the floor. They were called throw rugs for a reason, she had told one of her many overnight guests.

Two stripped bike frames, a dozen wheels minus their tires, several boxes of components, and a variety of other biking gear created an obstacle course Shannon stepped around before she reached a crowded bookshelf. It took several minutes for her to find what she was looking for—a thin, hardbound book a little larger than a legal pad at the bottom of a pile of other, much smaller books. Shannon loved to read and saved practically every book she had read. Every wall in the room was filled with bookcases containing hundreds of books ranging from lesbian fiction to the supernatural to home repair manuals.

The book weighed very little and just looking at the image of the majestic eagle soaring over a mountain filling the cover brought back memories. Shannon plopped into the worn recliner in the corner and hesitated before opening the dusty cover. She shouldn't, she told herself. Don't go down memory lane without a map. Or at least a plan to get back out. Ignoring her inner voice, she opened the book to the familiar page.

The picture of Caroline was so clear it was as if Shannon was looking at the real thing. A baseball cap pulled low on her head partially obscured her face but not enough that you couldn't see the twinkle of mischief in the dark eyes, the slight scar above the left eyebrow, a freckle just below her right cheekbone. She was laughing, her teeth perfectly straight and blistering white. Shannon knew Caroline's hair was shoulder length, but in this picture it was pulled back and through the opening in the back. This time the soaring eagle was embroidered on the front of the cap.

The picture didn't do her justice. Actually, since her picture was with all the other graduating seniors she was really more a young woman than a girl. A very sexy, sensuous woman. And all woman. Staring back at Shannon was her first *real* girlfriend. Not one of the girls she had fiddled around with in the backseat of a car or the last row in a movie theater. Each time they were together it was as if one moment she was floating on air, then riding a roller coaster the next. Shannon remembered how completely out of her mind she was for Caroline. She thought about her when they weren't together, and the last thing at night, and when they were able to sneak away for some together time, she was totally focused on her and only her.

Shannon often thought she was in love with her. She was a girl with the perfect family, the knockout body, and the intelligence to match. But she also scared the holy hell out of her. Caroline challenged her in ways Shannon didn't think possible. She made her think and stretch her imagination. She made it safe for Shannon to dream. The sex was incredible, as sex is when you're seventeen, but it was everything else about her that drove Shannon to carelessness when it came to her. That same carelessness was how she felt going down the mountain with nothing between her and the jagged rocks and trees below but her skill and nerve.

Shannon had tried not to think about Caroline over the years. Their paths intersected more often than she cared but not as much as they could have. She competed on the European circuit while Caroline had remained on the American tour. When their schedules did coincide, by some unspoken agreement, they were both careful not to cross too closely. What would she say if they had? What would she say to Caroline Davis if she really took the chance?

Chapter Four

The plane touched down in Montreal forty-five minutes late. Caroline grabbed her backpack from under the seat in front of her and prepared to wait while the other one hundred eighty-nine passengers jockeyed for position in the narrow aisle. She could understand those that had to make connections and, thankfully, she wasn't one of them. After almost six hours of traveling she wasn't quite to her final destination of the first race of the series but was close enough to still be in a hurry.

When the crowd thinned Caroline stood, careful not to bang her head on the overhead compartment. She had done that twice on this trip; the second time a nasty curse shot out of her mouth before she had a chance to stop it.

After stopping at the ladies room, Caroline followed the signs to baggage claim. The carousel for her flight had not yet started to spin, and her fellow passengers were standing three deep in anticipation of their bags passing within reach. She heard her name being called and turned to see a man in his twenties dressed in cargo shorts and a T-shirt with the phrase "I went down on Mount Brome" in red letters across his impressive chest. He was holding a handmade sign with her last name on it, signaling to Caroline he was her ride.

"Over here, I'm Caroline Davis," she called after raising her hand. The look on the man's face turned from one of bored acceptance to immediate interest. Caroline cringed. She had seen that look many times. At five foot five inches, her muscular body caught more than her share of attention from both sexes. Sometimes she was flattered, proud of what her hard work had produced, and other times she was just plain disinterested. Since the looker was a six foot male, this was definitely one of those times. The forty-five-minute drive to the mountain was going to feel much longer than that.

"*Mademoiselle Davis, bienvenue à Montréal. Je suis votre pilote Jacque.* Welcome to Montreal. I am Jacque, your driver." He repeated in English with more than a touch of a French accent.

"Thank you," Caroline replied. Her French was practically nonexistent, but she had picked up on his greeting. When she replied, his eyes betrayed his interest and she groaned to herself. The last thing she needed was to have to dodge a suitor.

"Let me take that for you," he said in English. "Do you have other bags?"

"Yes, I have two and a bicycle carrier."

A voice overhead told the waiting crowd that their luggage was now available on carousel twelve. A moment later a buzzer sounded and bags of all sizes and colors started spitting out of the conveyor belt tumbling onto the circling carousel.

"Mine are blue hard case with stickers of bikes on them." Caroline had learned early in her traveling career to make her bags as distinct as possible. It never ceased to amaze and irritate her when people could not identify their own luggage. She shook her head as a man practically took out several other waiting passengers while attempting to read the small luggage tag on a bag as it passed by.

"There is one of them," Jacque said drawing her attention back to the luggage moving by. He stepped forward and retrieved her suitcase, lifting it as if it were filled with feathers instead of her biking gear. No matter how little she packed, her helmet, knee pads, shin guards, and chest protector took up most of the room and she needed two bags to contain all her gear. Jacque snagged the second bag.

"We must go to the other side for your bicycle carrier, mademoiselle. The oversize bags are not delivered here."

"Yes, I know," she snapped more sharply than she intended and immediately softened her voice. "It's over there, isn't it?" She pointed to the far side of the baggage claim area. God, she was irritable. Maybe she needed a nap, or a good night's sleep. Maybe she just needed to stop thinking about Shannon Roberts. But that was easier said than done as she scanned every face in the area for the one that had tormented and teased her dreams for years.

Sitting in the second row of seats in the van, her bags and bike stacked neatly in the rear, Caroline dodged Jacque's attempt to make conversation. Finally, he got the message she wasn't interested in him or his chatter and he turned his focus on the road in front of them. As he drove, she didn't even pretend to observe the passing countryside on her way to Brodale, a tourist destination well known for its downhill skiing in the winter and for being the host of the first race in the mountain bike championship series. Caroline let her mind drift to Shannon.

They would run into each other again sometime during this race. They had to. They were competing in the same event, would attend some of the same sponsor events and mingle with the same people. Shit, she thought, there was a good chance they'd be standing next to each other in first and second place on the winner's stand.

The last time they were together was in Boulder for the U.S. Downhill Championships. They had managed to avoid each other most of the three days of the event, but occasionally their paths crossed. They were polite and civil, exchanging a few inconsequential words, but nothing of real importance. The last time they had said anything even remotely meaningful was that day more than ten years ago.

❖

Shannon tipped the bellman and dropped her backpack on the bed. She needed to unpack, shower, eat, and blow off some of her nervous energy, but not necessarily in that order. She glanced around the spacious room and didn't think twice about the size, the amenities, or the sheer luxury of the suite. She always traveled first class whether for her own personal pleasure or because her endorsement contract stipulated it. She had more money than most. At twenty-two, she'd inherited a large chunk of money from a trust fund set up by her great-aunt and it was doubled when she hit twenty-five. In two years when she reached thirty, it would double again.

Great-Aunt Martha had been a lesbian long before it was okay to be out. Everyone in the family thought she was simply a spinster schoolteacher, but one look at her pictures and Shannon knew otherwise.

She barely remembered the woman; she'd died when Shannon was eight, but according to her mother, Great-Aunt Martha had spent several summers with them when Shannon was small. She must have been able to tell that Shannon was going to be a lesbian even at her young age. Why else would she leave millions of dollars to a great-niece she barely knew?

Shannon stripped, left her clothes where they fell, and stepped into the shower. Her intent was to wash off the travel grime, slip into something that said "I'm showing you mine, now you show me yours," and go out on the town after the sponsors' meet and mingle tonight. She had been keyed up about this race more than usual and she knew why. "Caroline."

The name slipped off her tongue and into the steam with very little effort, but the effect caught Shannon by surprise. Her breath stuck in her throat, her nipples tightened under the bar of soap, and the point between her legs began to throb insistently.

She would see Caroline sometime in the next week and the thought never ceased to arouse her. She closed her eyes remembering. The feel of her touch, the softness of her lips, the smooth skin in that special place where her thighs joined the rest of her body. And that voice. The sound of her own name drifting off Caroline's lips at that moment when they were one was the sound music tried to imitate.

The memory evoked long dormant emotions, and Shannon's hands floated over her body as she fantasized about the time they had sex in the shower. It was the summer between their junior and senior year. They both had stayed at Mount Holyfield after most of the girls had gone home for the ten-week break. Shannon's parents were touring Europe, and Caroline was doubling up on courses hoping it would ensure her acceptance at Columbia.

Shannon entered the locker room after finishing a grueling tennis match against the local pro. She hadn't beat him, but she had come damn near close this time. If that gorgeous woman in the tight shorts hadn't walked by when she had, she would have caught up to his drop shot. Instead, she was left flat-footed with her mouth practically hanging open and he had won the set and the match.

Sweat droplets dripped off her hair and her clothes were plastered against her body as she approached the locker. The humidity in

Connecticut was brutal this time of the year and every inch of her was wet. Unlocking the small door, she heard a sound to her left and after drying off her face with her towel, turned to see a gorgeous girl standing not fifteen feet from her. When she looked again Shannon realized that the girl was actually one of her classmates.

Caroline Davis was in several of her classes and they had exchanged a few words now and then and were lab partners for a semester. They were both involved in mountain bike racing and had raced against each other for the past year, but were on different teams. Shannon was in heaven, getting the opportunity to stand close to the hottest girl in school, but Caroline always backed off when Shannon tried to become more than simply friendly. Lesbianism was taboo at the all-girls school, but those that were knew those that were and sex happened in their rooms, closets, empty classrooms, and any other place two young, horny teenagers could find. It was in the deserted locker room when Shannon made her move.

They had danced around their attraction with words and sly looks until Shannon finally took control. Caroline was wrapped in a towel and headed to the showers unaware that Shannon was on her heels. When she stepped inside the private enclosure, Shannon followed.

Caroline's eyes went wide with surprise then turned dark, something Shannon came to recognize as desire. When she reached behind her back to lock the thin metal door, Caroline reached for her. As if it had been choreographed, they came together with lips, hands, fingers, and heat. Shannon spun around, pinning Caroline against the door with her body. Breasts slid against breasts, thighs scissored together, and Shannon could not get enough of the girl who had been the object of her dreams and the source of her frustration for months.

Caroline's body was every bit as soft and firm as she had imagined. Her curves were curvy, her muscles hard and defined, and those special womanly places warm and silky. Caroline grabbed her head and pulled her closer when Shannon's mouth circled one nipple, then the other. She licked and sucked and ravaged the flesh with passion she never knew she had. She almost came when Caroline said her name.

The banging of a door reminded Shannon that they were not alone and she dragged her mouth off the luscious, full breasts. Quickly turning on the water to drown the sounds of their adventure, she pulled them both into the warm water. Caroline was shorter than she was by about four inches, and when she wrapped her arms around Shannon's neck and rose up on her toes, Shannon grabbed her ass with both hands and lifted her. Caroline got the message and locked her legs around her waist. Shannon bent her knees slightly to support them both.

Shannon's hand slid down Caroline's ass and one finger slid easily into her. Caroline took control of her own pleasure and Shannon remembered holding on for the ride. Grinding her crotch into Shannon's stomach, Caroline's breasts were inches from Shannon's mouth and she was not going to let that opportunity go by. Alternately sucking and biting each nipple and sliding her finger in and out of her pussy in tempo to Caroline's thrusting, it wasn't long before she felt Caroline stiffen, freeze for just an instant, then climax.

Wave after wave of pleasure rocked through Caroline and Shannon felt every spasm. They were sharing the same experience as if they were one. Shannon's legs gave out long before Caroline stopped gasping for breath. As much as she didn't want to, Shannon had to let her down. Caroline's soft legs slid down hers until her feet were on the ground, her still pulsing clitoris pressed against Shannon's thigh.

The laws of physics and lesbianism were such that Caroline's position put Shannon's clitoris in direct contact with what she needed to release the pressure inside her that was ready to explode. Caroline must have sensed her hardness because she quickly became the aggressor giving Shannon as much as she got.

Caroline's mouth was on her neck, her lips, her breasts, and Shannon didn't know whether to breathe or die. The steam from the water enveloped them like a warm mist. Caroline's hands roamed her body, often replaced with her lips and teeth as she navigated her way south. Shannon shuddered at the loss of contact against her clit, but when she realized Caroline's destination, thrust her hips to meet her.

Shannon let her head drop back, savoring the sensation of Caroline's mouth between her legs. Caroline's tongue flicked over her clit and Shannon grabbed her hair to keep her there. Faster and faster Caroline flicked, sucked, and licked driving Shannon out of her mind. Her orgasm started soft like the water cascading over her face but climaxed like Niagara Falls, rushing over the edge. She didn't know if she screamed, whispered, or was completely quiet and really didn't care. If anyone heard her she would be happy to accept the consequences.

The sound of her own voice echoing off the marble walls in the shower of Room 454 in the Chateau Brodale brought Shannon back to the present. Her body felt as it had that time long ago. Her breathing was rapid, her pulse racing, legs weak, head spinning. She pulled her fingers from between her legs and collapsed on the seat at the end of the enclosure. Catching her breath, Shannon realized what was missing. Her body was satisfied and full, but because she was alone in the shower, she was empty.

❖

The van pulled into the winding drive of the Gite Sur la Bonne Piste, a quaint bed and breakfast located at the base of Mount Brome, or Mont Bro as the locals called it. The house was typical Canadian style with a wide front porch, large windows framing either side of the massive oak front door, and three dormer windows peeking out from the high-pitched roof. The drive was crushed granite and crunched under Caroline's shoes as she walked to the back of the van to retrieve her bike case.

Rarely did she let anyone carry her bike, preferring to handle the oversize hard case that contained her livelihood herself. The case was fairly easy to maneuver despite its awkwardness, but she depended on its contents that could not easily be replaced. Caroline extended the handle on the black carrier and pulled it behind her up the narrow walkway.

The sign on the front door read *Come In* in bold cursive burned into a wooden plank. It felt odd not to knock upon entering a house that was not her own, but she reminded herself this was a B&B as she moved into the large front room.

The room was decorated in rustic style with antiques, handcrafts, and paintings giving the room, a cozy, lived-in feel. She had her choice of staying at one of the local hotels but preferred the privacy of the B&B to the noise and commotion she knew would exist in the hotels hosting the other riders.

A stand in one corner of the foyer was filled with colorful umbrellas while a coat rack was mounted on the wall to her left. The hardwood floors gleamed up at her while the thick wool runner muffled her footsteps.

"I'll be right there," a strong female voice said from the room to her right, and Caroline set her bike case directly under a picture of a snow-covered mountain. As corny as it seemed, the house smelled like fresh-baked cookies.

"Hello, you must be Caroline. I'm Beatrice. Welcome to the cottage," the woman said practically in one breath.

"Yes, I am, thank you." Caroline took the hand offered to her.

"Well, come with me and we'll get you checked in and settled in no time. Just leave your stuff by the door. Michael will bring it up to your room promptly. You're one of the riders?" Beatrice nodded toward the large case.

"Yes, I am." Caroline repeated her earlier answer. "You have a lovely place here." She followed Beatrice across the room. The craftsmanship of the woodwork was evident in the crown molding at the ceiling and on the winding staircase that led to what she assumed were the rooms upstairs.

"Thank you. Michael and I had been thinking of turning the house into a B-and-B for years and in 2002 we took the plunge. It's our dream come true, you might say."

Caroline could hardly imagine transforming your personal home into a type of rooming house where you have to make breakfast for everyone every day, make sure the bathrooms were clean all the time, and where strangers roamed through your house of their own free will as a dream come true, as Beatrice phrased it. To her, it sounded like a pain in the ass that could very easily turn into a nightmare.

Within ten minutes she was in her room, her luggage at the foot of the bed, her bike case against the wall by the closet. Shaking off the memories of Shannon that had dogged her for the past few days, Caroline unpacked, put her clothes neatly into the tall dresser in the corner, and the contents of her backpack on the small desk. She inspected her safety gear for any damage that might have occurred in transit. She brought with her one helmet, one chest guard, two pairs of shoes, a pair of elbow and knee pads, and assorted bike shorts, shirts, and socks. If she damaged or lost anything else, she could replace it from any one of the numerous vendor stands that would fill the expo area at each event.

Reaching for her iPod, her attention was drawn to a magazine lying neatly at the right hand corner of the desk. It was the program for the race, and Caroline's breath caught in her throat as she recognized the image that adorned the cover. She didn't need to read the caption that identified the rider as *Shannon Roberts—Babe of Brodale*. She was soaring over a jump with at least five feet of air between her tires and the rocky ground beneath. Her face was set in concentration, legs bent at the knees, elbows flexed, riding high in the saddle as she accelerated into the jump.

Caroline couldn't help herself and she opened the first page of the magazine. There would be more pictures of Shannon inside and she wasn't disappointed to see her on the second and fifth page as well. But it was the back cover that made her knees weak and the glossy pages shake in her hands. Shannon was standing in front of her bike, feet crossed at the ankles, arms across her chest. Her mouth was formed into an almost smirk but had just enough smile to be beguiling.

Her bike shorts fit her like a second skin, slim hips with strong, muscular thighs jutting out below them. Caroline knew those calves were rock solid; at least they were years ago, and they looked like they had only gotten firmer. Her fingers tingled as she remembered how smooth the skin was and how the hard muscle quivered under her touch. Mussed blond hair reminded her of how it looked after she ran her hands through it. Or grabbed it to hold Shannon's head and mouth tight to her.

"Shit, shit, shit," she exclaimed louder with each word. She had allowed Shannon to get to her again. And this time it was a simple set of pictures. What would it be like when she saw her in the flesh? Something told her it wouldn't be long before she would find out.

CHAPTER FIVE

Caroline tossed the magazine on the bed and ducked into the shower—a cold shower. She knew Shannon would be featured in any material advertising the race. Not only was she one of the best downhill racers in the world, she was the media darling of the circuit. The cameras loved her, she always had a quip for the reporters, and she made absolutely no secret that she preferred to spend her off hours with the female groupies versus the male. Shannon Roberts was *the* draw at every event.

The fact that Shannon received all the attention didn't bother Caroline. In fact, she was glad it wasn't her. Where Shannon's talent came naturally, Caroline had to work hard for everything she had. She needed to focus before each race, preferring a few hours of solitude to the massive throngs of fans clambering for her autograph. She had a reputation for being aloof in the days leading up to the race but relaxed and approachable after.

She dressed for the sponsor's event, grabbed her room key, and headed down the stairs. There were several people sitting in the living room that Caroline assumed were other guests, and she nodded as she passed by on her way to the front door. The reception was being held about a mile away and the walk would do her good.

As she approached the event hall the sounds of music, loud voices, and clinking glasses drifted through the clear evening sky. It was cool but not so much that she needed a jacket, the long sleeves of her shirt providing enough warmth. Taking a deep breath to calm her racing pulse, Caroline stepped inside.

Shannon was talking to another rider and she glanced up just as Caroline entered the room. Everyone in the room must have stopped talking at once because the only thing Shannon heard was the thudding of her heart. My God, she's just as hot as ever, she thought as Caroline hesitated just inside. She watched Caroline glance around the room as if looking for a familiar face to run to. Shannon knew what Caroline's reaction had been every time she saw her. She would turn and leave the room. But Shannon wasn't ready to stop looking at the woman who played her body like a classical guitar those many years ago, so she excused herself and found a more secluded position for her observations.

Caroline was dressed in a knee-length khaki skirt and sandals. From experience, Shannon knew that Caroline's pale blue shirt would bring out the color of her eyes. Her hair was tucked behind her ears, and other than a pair of earrings that sparkled in the bright lights, a big, clunky sport watch was the only other jewelry she wore.

Snagging another glass of champagne from a passing waiter, Shannon watched Caroline work her way around the room. She stopped and chatted with sponsors, the media, and other riders. An unfamiliar jolt of jealousy jabbed in her gut when two of the riders made a play for her. Caroline appeared to humor them, and after a few moments slid out of their circle and walked in the direction of the patio. Shannon followed.

The sound dimmed when Shannon closed the door behind her. Caroline turned. Her face was an expression of curiosity, shock, desire, and hurt, one right after the other. Shannon couldn't take her eyes off her. She hadn't been this alone with her in years, and it was as if it were only this afternoon that they had been this close. Caroline looked like she was going to flee, so Shannon spoke.

"Hello, Caroline. You're looking well."

Caroline's mouth opened and closed twice before anything came out. "Hello, Shannon. I expected to see you this week. How are you?" Caroline shifted her weight and took a sip of her drink.

The voice was slightly huskier than she remembered, but Shannon would know it anywhere. Especially in the dark. "I'm fine, thanks." Her brain stopped working and Shannon's ability for witty small talk went with it. She had no idea what she wanted to say to Caroline. Ultimately, she knew they would see each other this week, or the next, or the one after that. She had not thought that they wouldn't have to say something to each other, but now that it was here, she was speechless. By the look on Caroline's face, she was as well.

Shannon felt her feet move, and before she knew it, she was standing beside Caroline looking into the dark Montreal sky. The stars winked at her as if to say they knew she had the prettiest woman at the party.

"You're riding for TKS." Caroline broke the silence.

"Yes, I guess you could say they made me an offer I couldn't refuse." TKS was the world's leading manufacturer of bicycle frames and their sponsorship was coveted. They treated their riders like gold and paid them almost as much.

"So I hear," Caroline replied with a lightness in her voice that Shannon hadn't expected. "Your picture is everywhere."

"Yeah, well," Shannon stammered. "You know how it is." She liked being the center of attention but felt uncomfortable about it now.

"Yeah." Caroline had sponsors and knew the drill.

"How's the leg?" Shannon asked looking at the bare leg not far from hers.

"Better than new."

The clenching in her gut reminded Shannon of how she felt when she found out Caroline had taken a nasty fall eighteen months ago. At twenty-nine, Shannon hadn't been sick a day in her life other than the occasional mild cold or flu. By the grace of God, or just sheer luck, she had managed to avoid serious injury during the ten years and thousands of miles of mountain bike riding she had under her belt. Actually, under her butt was a more fitting description, but it was the same nonetheless.

"I was sorry to hear about it." Shannon cringed at her useless words. A fellow rider had called to tell her about Caroline's accident assuming she would be thrilled that her major competitor would be out of the running for quite some time and said as much. Shannon had jumped down the messenger's throat for gloating over something that was very serious. She hadn't heard much about Caroline's recovery, and other than the fading scar that snaked down the outside of her right leg, Caroline seemed to be as fine as she had said.

Caroline laughed. "You should have heard it on my end."

Shannon's heart skidded to a stop at the sound of the rich laughter. Memories flooded her brain and her body and she was suddenly very hot.

"Must have hurt like hell." Shannon shuddered.

Caroline smiled at the simple statement and it was her turn to shudder at the memories and she had plenty of them. "Only when I was awake. Which was all the time because it hurt like hell," she added. "But I'm ready for Brodale."

Caroline had done her research on the mountain she was bound and determined to conquer. Ski Brodale had set up three new courses on the Versant du Lac site specifically for the event. The material she read said the downhill course was filled with rocky outcroppings, wooded sections, and abrupt descents. The material went on to say that "many tight corners, jumps, and other obstacles will follow one another to create a course with a difficulty level that even the hardiest downhill kamikazes can scarcely imagine." She had competed in several smaller races leading up to the championship series to dust off the cobwebs and get back in the groove of being in the saddle, but she wanted this win, her first big race after her first big injury.

"I'm sorry you had to go through that," Shannon said quietly.

Caroline turned to face her. Shannon had aged gracefully and where once a gangly teenager stood was now an accomplished, successful woman. Her hair was in its usual style of disarray, the familiar liquid blue eyes were clear and focused directly on her. What could Shannon ever be sorry for? Sorry to hear about my fall? Sorry that we'll be competing against each other? Sorry that you ran out on me, left me standing all alone on that warm afternoon so many years ago?

Finishing her drink, Caroline pushed those thoughts out of her mind. It was over ten years ago, for crying out loud. They were teenagers. Stupid, impulsive teenagers whose recklessness caught up with them one warm spring day. Silence filled the air between them.

"I have to get back inside." Caroline used her glass to indicate the party going full force on the other side of the doors. "People to see, hands to shake, elbows to rub. You know." She ended using the same phrase Shannon had a few moments ago. "It was good to see you again, Shannon. Good luck this week."

And before she could say something she might regret later, Caroline opened the doors and walked through leaving that part of her life behind—again.

❖

"Where're ya going, baby?"

The question grated on Shannon's last nerve. It wasn't so much what was asked but the fact that it was asked at all. Shannon bit back a caustic reply. What she really wanted to say was, "This was just a fuck. We fucked. It's over. I'm leaving. Simple, simple, simple. It's not rocket science." But she didn't. It wasn't... Shit, she didn't even know the woman's name. It wasn't her fault she was in such a crappy mood. When Caroline left her on the patio earlier tonight, a rage came over her like she had never experienced. She was so angry with herself for letting Caroline get to her. The fact that she had no idea she still had feelings for her was one thing, but to let her get under her smooth finish was something that would never happen again.

"I'm going back to my hotel," she answered pulling on her shorts and looking around the dark room for her shirt. She found it on the other side of the room by the door. She slipped her sandals on and forced herself not to run across the room, grab her shirt, and jet out the door. More calm than she felt, Shannon buttoned her shirt and when she was at the halfway point, reached for the doorknob. "Thanks, take care," she mumbled on her way out the door.

The hall was brightly lit in direct contrast to the blackness she felt swim over her. Rarely had she felt slimy and cheap after leaving a woman's bed, but it was all over her now. She had used that woman to get over her feelings for Caroline, and her conscience was creeping up on her. She never used one woman to get over another. Well, maybe *used* wasn't an accurate word. She had slept with a few women to exorcise a demon or two from inside her, but it was always a mutually pleasurable event. But not this time. She was rough, straight to the point, and maybe a little bit mean. The woman didn't seem to mind; she actually preferred it. But it did nothing for Shannon. She was dry as a bone and could barely finish what she had started.

After Caroline had left, she had returned to the party with a chip on her shoulder and an attitude that said "take me as I am or go fuck yourself." Her sponsors loved it. They had hired her reputation of an almost bad girl who just happened to be the best biker in the world. The fact that she had the body to back up that attitude was a significant bonus.

The woman had caught her eye while Shannon was ordering her fourth Crown and Coke. It was taking more and more alcohol lately to be interested, and on more than one occasion had crossed the fine line between just enough and too much. The bartender was pouring the drinks strong, and between an empty stomach and seeing Caroline again, she was definitely feeling the effects of the alcohol. She and the woman had barely spoken before Shannon was dragging her to the elevator and up to her room. Shannon preferred to go to the woman's place when she had sex, enabling her to leave when she wanted to. She wasn't very good with tactfully telling her sex partner to go.

Dawn was breaking when Shannon pushed the revolving door and stepped outside. The air was heavy and it felt like rain. Great, just what she needed, to slog through the rain on her practice runs with a whiskey and woman hangover. How did she get here? One minute she was sipping champagne and making nice with sponsors, the next she was making a dash for the nearest exit. For heaven's sake, it wasn't like she'd never run into an ex before. They were scattered all over the U.S., more than a few around the world.

What was it about Caroline that continued to rub at her? They were together when they were teenagers. When they didn't know any better. Shit, when they didn't know anything about life and how to get through it. It was a childhood thing. So why did it creep up on her at the most inopportune times and fuck her up so much?

Shannon stopped at the first place that served coffee and bought the largest serving they had. She took her coffee black and strong and this brew was perfect. She walked out of the cool shop sipping her hot beverage, confused over her body's reaction to Caroline. Again and again, the memory of their last time together was the freshest, sweetest, and the most painful.

It was a hot day similar to what she expected today was going to be. She was in Caroline's room at MHA; they were studying for their calculus exam the next day. It was four weeks before graduation and Caroline needed to pass this test and the final. Like most things, school came easily for Shannon, especially math and the sciences, but Caroline had struggled from the first crack of the thick math book.

Caroline worked hard and studied even harder to understand the complicated methods, statistics, and ridiculous formulas. She memorized, developed her own form of remembering symbols, and was still eking her way to a passing grade—barely.

They had been at it for several hours when Shannon sensed she was being watched. Her suspicions were confirmed when she glanced up and found Caroline looking at her. She recognized that look. It was the one that set her heart to race, her blood to pound, and her clit to throb.

"What are you doing?" she asked, knowing full well what the answer was going to be.

"Nothing," was the answer.

"Why do I not believe you?" Caroline's eyes sparked with challenge at her follow-up question.

"Whatever do you mean?" Her voice was thick and smooth.

Caroline didn't move any closer, but it suddenly felt warmer in the room and Shannon's throat was dry.

"You should be studying." Shannon's protest was weak.

"I am." Caroline licked her lips.

Shannon suddenly found it hard to breathe. Caroline was looking at her as if she were memorizing every contour of her body. Her eyes moved up and down her with agonizing slowness over those parts that were hidden under her clothes. Her nipples tightened when Caroline lingered on her chest, and Shannon could have sworn they traced the MHA letters on her shirt.

"You're not going to pass if you don't pay attention to what you're doing."

Caroline's sweet, sexy smile slid over her very kissable mouth.

"Speaking of paying attention," she said, making sure Shannon knew she was referring to her erect nipples.

"Caroline." Shannon tried to sound scolding, but it came out more of a plea than a command.

"Yes?" was the sweet reply.

"Stop," was her equally pathetic reply.

"Is that what you really want? Do you want me to stop looking at you? Stop caressing your body in my mind? Stop remembering how soft your skin is, how strong your legs are when they're wrapped around me? How good you taste? Do you want me to stop making love to you in my head?"

Caroline paused. Shannon knew she should say yes. Caroline needed her to be strong and help her focus, but she was only seventeen, for crying out loud. Her libido and insatiable lust for the girl sitting across the room from her ruled her life.

"Yes."

Caroline raised her eyebrows in obvious surprise. "Yes?"

"Yes. I want you to stop caressing me in your mind, stop remembering how soft my skin is, how strong my legs are when they're wrapped around you, and how good I taste. I want you to stop making love to me in your head and get over here and do it to me." Shannon was so turned on she could hardly stand it. It only took a look from Caroline to set her off, but to hear her say what was on her mind took her to another world entirely.

With excruciating deliberateness, Caroline closed the distance between them. Their rooms were small so it wasn't far, but it seemed like an eternity until Caroline covered her lips with hers.

Caroline had an amazing mouth and often times kissed Shannon until she was completely senseless. This kiss was soft and tender, hesitating between light nibbles and nips on her lips. No part of their body was touching except their mouths and Shannon's body was on fire as much as if Caroline had her hands all over it.

Shannon couldn't stand it any longer and pulled Caroline onto her lap. The familiar weight of her was comforting, and every time they came together she was amazed how perfectly their bodies fit together.

Soft, exploring, arousing kisses turned to hard, heated passion and Shannon couldn't get Caroline's clothes off fast enough. The need to feel Caroline's skin on hers was unbearable. Giving up, she simply pushed Caroline's shirt up and latched her mouth to exposed breasts.

Caroline grabbed her head and pulled her closer and moaned when she took her nipple into her mouth. "Yes," she said on the trailing end of a sigh. Shannon gave the other breast equal attention and soon Caroline was arching her hips in the universal signal for touch.

Shannon slipped her hand into the waistband of her shorts and down the familiar path to the warmth that awaited her. It was her turn to moan this time when her fingers easily slid into the waiting flesh. Caroline was an exquisite lover, wet and inviting, always ready for her. She rocked against the pressure of Shannon's hand and Shannon almost lost control.

It drove Shannon crazy when Caroline took control of her own pleasure. There was just something about the way she moved, seeking the pressure she wanted, the touch she desired, the release she needed that often took Shannon over the edge. This time was no different and when she felt Caroline's clit grow hard and start to twitch under her fingers she pulled her tighter. Caroline rocked and bucked against her as her fingers worked their magic for both of them.

Caroline straddled her lap, arms wrapped around her neck, her back to the door. Shannon's mouth feasted on Caroline's breasts and they both were completely oblivious to the audience standing in the now open doorway as they came together.

A gasp that was not theirs caused Caroline to raise her head. Shannon felt the movement, but it was the sudden freezing of the body on top of her that got her attention. She released Caroline's nipple and blinked several times to regain her focus. When Caroline still had not moved, Shannon turned her head to see what had her attention. With her fingers still deep inside Caroline and her breathing ragged, she looked into the stern eyes of the Dean of Mount Holyfield Academy. Standing next to her was Caroline's father, his face beet red with rage.

❖

The scene was every lesbian's nightmare. Between the shouting, recriminations, shock, embarrassment, anger, and a good dose of absolute terror, Caroline and Shannon were somehow able to pull themselves together, straighten their clothes, and stand to face the two people that were now judge and jury. And judge them they did.

"Get out," were the only words Caroline's father said. His tone was quiet and menacing with barely controlled furor.

"Mr. Davis, I can explain—" Shannon began.

"I don't need an explanation, young lady. I saw what was going on. What you were doing to my daughter."

"Daddy, Shannon was—"

"I know what Shannon was doing," he snapped.

Shannon stepped forward trying to make her point. "Mr. Davis, I—"

Steven Davis stepped forward until they were almost nose-to-nose. Shannon was either too stupid or too brave to back away.

"You had your hands on my daughter. Your filthy hands were—"

"Daddy, stop it," Caroline shouted cutting through the tension hanging in the air. "Shannon wasn't doing anything to me that I didn't want her to. This isn't the way I wanted you to find out, but this is who I am. I'm a lesbian and I was a lesbian long before Shannon came into my life."

"Get her out of here before I kill her," Davis said to no one specific. It was Dean Phillips who jumped at the command.

"Ms. Roberts, go to your room and wait for me." Her tone was as frightening in its simplicity as Caroline's father's had been.

The next few days were a complete blur for Shannon. Her roommate was reassigned, she was forbidden to leave her room, and her parents were called. She was allowed to take her final exams in the library away from the other students and as soon as she was finished, forced to leave the campus. She had not been allowed to see or speak with Caroline before she left.

She tried to stand up for Caroline but couldn't. Didn't she need to defend Caroline? It wasn't Caroline's fault. Shannon had started it all the day in the locker room. God, that seemed like a lifetime ago.

Her parents shipped her off to Switzerland for the summer with strict instructions to not contact Caroline. They were not quite as shocked as Steven Davis, but then again they didn't walk in and see another girl's fingers up their daughter's snatch.

She tried to call Caroline several times, but the line was always picked up by her parents. Mutual friends passed on information, and once or twice Shannon was able to get through but only to Caroline's voicemail. They talked once or twice, but it was awkward. They never regained the natural case they had with each other before her father walked in. Shannon did what she thought was best and left her alone. That was ten years, ten months, and a few odd days ago. But it seemed like yesterday.

CHAPTER SIX

Ladies and gentlemen, next up, riding for Bellow is number twenty-five, Caroline Davis."

The voice over the loudspeaker was practically drowned out by the cheers of the crowd around her. Caroline inched toward the starting line readying herself for the descent down one of Canada's most majestic and dangerous mountains. She tugged at her helmet, adjusted her elbow pads, tightened the Velcro on her riding gloves, and took a deep breath.

Focus, said the voice in her head. You can do this. It's a simple course you've been down half a dozen times already. You know where the turns are, the rocks, that one stump across the road about halfway down, the tight hairpin turn just before the long stretch to the finish line. It's just another race, like all the other races before.

Caroline repeated the mantra while the announcer finished reciting her stats, wins, and hometown. The red light was steady as the timer next to it counted down. When it got to fifteen, she rolled within centimeters of the infrared start line. At ten, she clipped her left shoe into the pedal. At five, she flexed her fingers over the brakes. Three, two, one. She shot out.

The first twenty yards were smooth and she pedaled hard, picking up speed. The trail veered sharply to the left and she navigated the change smoothly, picking up more speed on the flat downhill surface before the next obstacle. She flew up and down hills, over sharp rocks and boulders big enough to be trouble but small enough to be in the middle of the trail.

With her shoes clipped to her pedals, she was able to use both the downward motion of her legs as well as the upward for speed, jumps, and to maintain control. The only danger was that if she fell, she needed to twist her foot just right to release it or suffer a severe injury.

No, not now. Please not now. The familiar tightening of her chest, shortness of breath, the overwhelming need to flee unexpectedly washed over Caroline. She had no clue it was coming until it was right on top of her and there was little she could do to stop it.

It was the last thing she needed right now. She hadn't had a panic attack for months. They started the first time she was back on her bike after her devastating injury. At first, she didn't know what was going on. All she knew was that it scared the hell out of her. She felt like she was having a heart attack. Her legs were weak, her breathing much faster than normal. Her heart was racing, her throat dry. She couldn't get off her bike fast enough, and it was all she could do to get away.

She confided in her father what had happened and he accompanied Caroline to her doctor. After a battery of other tests, she was diagnosed with panic attacks and referred to a psychologist who was better equipped to help her deal with what was described as a form of posttraumatic stress syndrome. After a few sessions with Dr. Blackstone, Caroline had learned how to deal with the attacks through a series of calming techniques. She began them now.

Forcing herself to concentrate, she shifted her weight over her legs, jumping over a dip in the trail that would send a less experienced rider flying over the handlebars causing certain injury. The bike hit the ground, and between the shocks on the front and rear of her bike as well as the powerful muscles in her legs acting like springs, she hardly felt the return to earth.

She expertly conquered the twists and turns of the course gaining speed when she could, backing off when she had to. It seemed like only seconds before she saw the finish line to her left. The hairpin curve she was worried about was to her left. She braked going into the bend, her rear wheel skidding almost out from under her as she maneuvered through the tight turn. Cheers erupted when she emerged and she pedaled hard through the finish line.

Caroline skidded to a stop and looked over her shoulder at her time displayed on the Omega board. This was the first of the qualifying rounds. Each round consisted of two timed events, with the fastest racers moving on to the next round until only the final ten remained. The final round was three races, the combined time resulting in the winner of that leg of the championship. In addition to the blue jersey, the winner received fifteen points. Ten points went to the rider who finished second, five for third, and three for fourth. At the end of the race series, the rider with the highest number of points was declared the overall champion.

"Yes," Caroline shouted as her time and bib number flashed to the top of the standings. At 5:39:42, she was three seconds ahead of the second place rider. Caroline had been on the circuit long enough to know the racers, their strengths and weaknesses, and the five riders behind her could not beat her time. Except for the one that was coming down the mountain now.

In what seemed like an instant, Shannon breezed across the finish line and Caroline thought she was barely breathing hard. Her time was four seconds ahead of Caroline's and she and Shannon, along with eight others, moved on to the next round.

The remainder of the day continued in the same manner. By her last race, Caroline had ridden down the challenging hill seven times, each time faster than the last, her confidence gaining.

Her parents and Fran had arrived the night before and were cheering her on from the grandstand adjacent to the finish line. Steven and Robin Davis attended as many of her races as they could, but money was tight in the Davis household. But there was no way they'd miss this one. Fran's parents were so rich she was able to go pretty much wherever she wanted. Most of the time she chose to be with Caroline. Surprisingly, she had gotten to be a pretty good bike mechanic and an excellent chief cook and bottle washer.

Freshly showered, Caroline walked down the stairs and saw her parents already sitting in the living room of the B&B. They were engaged in conversation with an elderly gentleman who was doing most of the talking with his hands. The fact that he was speaking French and her parents didn't know a word didn't seem to stop him from carrying on his side of the conversation.

"Caroline," her mother said, obviously relieved at the interruption.

"Hey, Mom, is Fran down yet?"

"Yes, she's outside with one of the men working on the yard, or trimming the bushes or something." Her mother waved her hand in the direction of the front of the house. "Why don't we go find her?"

Caroline chuckled at how smoothly her mother made their escape from the man who had turned his attention and antics to the woman to his left. They stepped outside. The stickiness of the past few days had subsided leaving crisp, cool mountain air. The three of them walked around the building and Caroline saw Fran in a casual pose leaning against a fence gate. She was talking to a tall man with hair the color of coal and by the look on his face, she was working her magic.

"Speaking of romance," her father said. Her parents had heard enough stories and been around Fran long enough to know what she was up to. "Are you seeing anyone?"

After the debacle in high school with Shannon, her parents finally came to grips with the fact that Caroline was not simply going through a phase brought on by attending an all-girls school. After four years at Columbia and three more getting her graduate degree, they were closer than most of her friends were with their parents.

"Not really." Caroline couldn't very well say that she had a torrid night with a near stranger a week ago. She could tell her parents anything, but she drew the line at her sex life.

"Not really or no?" her mother said. Caroline had four siblings, each married and some with children of their own, but her mother still worried about her. When she became a mother, Caroline supposed she would as well.

"Not really. Really," she said to counter the look of skepticism on her mother's face. "I've gone out a few times but nothing serious. I've been training, remember?" She nudged her mother affectionately.

"How could I forget? You don't call and I can't remember the last time you came home for a visit. Little Clarice is walking now and you're going to miss it."

At the name of her latest niece, Caroline smiled. "Mom, I doubt Clarice is going to stop walking anytime soon. It's not a phase she's going through. I'm no child development expert, but I think she'll be doing that for the rest of her life." Caroline loved teasing her mother.

"You know what I mean, young lady. Don't get cheeky with me. Your father and I aren't getting any younger, you know."

"Mom," Caroline replied exasperated. "You're both only fifty-two. That's hardly pushing up daisy years." She gave her mom a quick hug. "But I know what you mean. This is my last season, and once I get my Ph.D. and get settled I'll be there so much you'll think I moved back in. Now let's rescue that man from Fran and get something to eat."

❖

The next morning Shannon's alarm buzzed incessantly. She didn't want to get up. She hadn't gone out drinking or partying with or without a sexy Canadian. She just didn't feel like getting out of bed, which was odd because today was the finals of this all-important first race and she was atop the leader board ahead of Caroline and a rookie from Spain.

It was seven thirty when she finally rolled out of bed. She hadn't slept well. Images of Caroline floated in and out of her dreams. In one, she was laughing, in another angry, in a third, she was making love to her, and finally, she was crying. Shannon couldn't quite figure out what was going on in each sequence, but she knew she was in all of them.

Dressed and washing down the remainder of her breakfast with an energy drink, Shannon closed and locked the door behind her. Her footsteps were silent on the plush carpet of the hall, the elevator barely making a sound as it opened its doors on her floor. The car was crowded and she recognized a few other riders as she stepped inside. A chorus of "good lucks" sent her on her way when they reached the hotel lobby.

It was a short ride to the race expo and riders' area, but Shannon opted to walk. Her start time for the first heat of the finals was after lunch and she was too keyed up to sit idly in the backseat of a cab. Her gear was safely secured in her sponsor's trailer so all she carried was her backpack.

She garnered more than a few passing looks as she walked down the street. At five foot six, she wasn't much taller or shorter than the other riders, but her shock of blond, almost white hair drew some attention. Most of the men and a fair number of women checked her out from the bold letters across her chest to the fitted bike shorts covering her muscular thighs.

As she neared the race venue, dozens of people wished her luck. She wasn't famous by any means, but she was well known on the circuit and by fans of the sport.

She entered the riders' only area and quickly scanned the grounds for Caroline. She would already be here, Shannon knew, checking out her gear, her bike, and getting psyched for the finals. Shannon was leading Caroline by only four seconds, which on this course was like a split second. One misstep, loss of concentration, or missed execution in a tight turn and the race could be lost.

Shannon never understood riders who had to meditate or get psyched up for a race. She simply imagined the trail in her mind, rode the lift to the top, and waited for her turn to descend. She never took it too seriously, which made her relaxed and fluid on the course. Usually, she won or came in second. Rarely did she come in anything lower than fourth, and she had not taken a spill in over three years.

Frank Striker, the owner of TKS, was waiting inside the trailer when Shannon entered. "There's my goldmine," he said before she even had the door closed behind her.

Shannon hated the perpetual leer on his face, but he never said or did anything that would give her the right to slap it off. He was her major sponsor. She sold her image, name, and reputation to him in exchange for big bucks. She hated the business side of racing but knew it was part of the game she had to play. She had money of her own, but why spend it when she could spend someone else's just as easily?

"Hey, Frank, how's it going?" Shannon asked as her way of saying good morning.

"Makin' money and makin' more money." Frank's middle name was greedy.

Shannon didn't reply but went straight to her bike. At times she felt more at home with her bike than she did with most people. The carbon, aluminum, rubber, and wire were an extension of her. A way to express herself, the excitement of life, her race toward the future. There had to be some Freudian hypothesis in it all, but she tried hard not to think that deep.

"You're gonna take home the blue jersey today, Shan, I can feel it. Davis can't catch you, and the rest of the field are all wannabes. I have money that you'll take it all this year. You know you're the favorite. Davis gets the sympathy vote 'cause of her broke leg, but she's got nothing compared to you."

There were many things that Shannon disliked about Frank Striker and he just about hit every one of them in his monologue. She hated being called Shan, his constant stroking of her ego was unnecessary and nauseating, and he never had a good thing to say about Caroline or any other rider.

She and Caroline were ranked number one and two in the world and she deserved, and had earned, the respect that went along with that. "Caroline is fully recovered. She has just as much chance to win this as I do. As anyone, for that matter."

"But she isn't going to get a million dollar bonus if she does, is she?"

Shannon bit her tongue on the first response that came to mind and chose the second instead. "Who knows? Maybe she will." The rest of her statement was drowned out by Frank's laugh.

"From Bellow? They're so cheap they squeak when you say their name. She probably barely got enough money to pay for the trip."

She wasn't in the mood to spar with Frank today so she picked up her gear and headed out the door followed by Frank's parting words. "Kick ass, girl!"

❖

Caroline pulled on her knee pads and buckled her shoes. The butterflies in her stomach were better than a clock. They always arrived about an hour before her start time and when she heard the announcement for the third heat she knew she had about forty-five minutes until she needed to be at the top of the hill.

Commotion behind her drew Caroline's attention and she turned just in time to see Shannon enter the staging area. She had a presence that made her seem much larger than her average size. She drew crowds wherever she went at races, and it was particularly evident today by the numbers of people the security guards made wait outside the gate.

Caroline knew every inch of Shannon's body, her mannerisms, her body gave away her moods, but that was years ago. God knew she was not the same person she was in high school and she suspected Shannon had changed as much as well. But the sense of familiarity, even after all these years, was unmistakable. Shannon still had the same swagger, the same sense of purpose, the same determined look in her eye she had when they were together.

Shannon gazed around the area, nodding to a few riders, looking past others, and Caroline watched Shannon's eyes settle on her. Her heartbeat double-timed once, then twice before settling into a faster than normal cadence. Shannon's expression immediately went blank but not before Caroline saw the moment of recognition and remembrance fill her face.

Caroline nodded and motioned Shannon over. With each step Shannon took toward her, Caroline's pulse raced a bit faster. Stay calm, she told herself. Don't let her get to you, she repeated in her head until Shannon stopped in front of her.

"I just wanted to wish you luck," Caroline managed to say more calmly than she felt.

Shannon hesitated as if she were deciding how to respond. Finally she said, "Thanks, you too. It's going be a tough one. The bobby pin about three-quarters down has gotten loose."

Caroline knew the spot Shannon was referring to. It was a tight turn where the hard-packed dirt had eroded away due to the dozens of tires skidding over its surface. Interesting that Shannon warned her about it.

"You're riding a Shimano crankset. How's that working for you?" Caroline asked wanting to keep the conversation going and Shannon close to her. This was the most they had spoken to each other since that awful day in her dorm room. Shannon looked surprised at the question.

"Good. They're pretty tight and smooth. I think it's their best crank yet."

The bike techno jargon was going on all around them and would the entire series. Each rider believed that what she was riding was the best and many an argument ensued when two vehemently disagreed.

"How is the Bellow working out for you?" Shannon asked referring to Caroline's frame manufacturer.

"Great. It's light but stronger than I've ever ridden. The control is everything it's touted to be." Caroline was surprised the conversation was going on as long as it had. For the past ten years, when she and Shannon were competing in the same race they kept their mutually agreed upon distance, rarely saying anything more than obligatory greetings to each other. It was an awkward yet comfortable arrangement at the same time.

"How are they to work with?"

The name of her major sponsor took the conversation to a slightly more personal level. "Great. Russ is an absolute professional and his team is constantly looking to improve the technology. They debrief me after every race, and when I just want to collapse in exhaustion they want to talk about pull, swag, and bend." Caroline couldn't help but smile at the image of the four tech geeks pumping her for information about how the bike handled.

Shannon looked like she wanted to say something else but instead wished her luck again and walked over to where her gear was stored. Caroline watched her back and noticed her shoulders were pulled back, her back straight, and the ass she had grabbed, squeezed, and devoured a lifetime ago was as delicious as ever.

❖

Caroline buckled her helmet, swung her leg over the seat, and adjusted her gloves. She gripped the handlebars and nodded. In a heartbeat, she was through the gate.

Her heart raced as the adrenaline she had kept at bay let loose. She forced herself to relax her grip, release the muscles in her legs, and simply enjoy the ride. The first turn was to the right. She sailed through it, rocketing over the rough terrain of the top third of the course. Her thighs absorbed the pounding of the uneven rocks bounding the bike beneath her while her upper body remained relatively smooth.

Caroline's torso was protected by the thick hard shell of a chest guard, her legs and arms protected from rocks and road rash if she had the misfortune to fall. Catching air over the first of two jumps, the cool mountain breeze whipped over her cheeks. Faster and faster she went, dodging rocks the size of basketballs, logs embedded in the hard dirt, and sand as soft as fresh snow. She never once lost control of her bike, her concentration, or her focus. Approaching the last turn, she remembered Shannon's warning and braked hard going into the turn. Her Kenda tires gripped the loose dirt and she accelerated out of the sharp elbow, up and over the last obstacle before the straightway to the finish.

She heard the cheers from the crowd, saw the sponsor signs flashing by as she pushed and pulled with her legs to cross the finish line. The crowd erupted when Caroline skidded to a stop and turned to look at her time. Her heart soared. She had beaten her own time by an astonishing five seconds. Her hands were shaking as she slid her goggles to the top of her helmet. Shannon had to beat her last run by four seconds to win and Caroline had no doubt that she could do it. Like any good competitor, she wished her a safe, albeit a much slower ride.

Her legs were like rubber as Caroline coasted out of the finish area. She was greeted with congratulations and slaps on the back as she exited toward the post-race staging area. She kept her eyes glued to the JumboTron, a gigantic video screen specially designed to view outdoors. Caroline didn't have to wait long for Shannon to begin her final run. As she approached the starting line, she nodded that she was ready and sprinted out of the gate.

Caroline's body involuntarily leaned along with Shannon as she conquered each obstacle. When Shannon jumped, she did, when she leaned back behind her saddle, Caroline did as well, and when Shannon's back wheel slid out from under her on the last hairpin turn, her stomach dropped. Shannon lost precious seconds on that error and Caroline practically held her breath as Shannon flew cross the finish line.

The crowd went wild and Caroline was enveloped with hugs from well-wishers. She had won the first race.

CHAPTER SEVEN

Shannon couldn't make it through the throng of people congratulating Caroline on her victory so she simply headed to the TKS trailer instead. The awards ceremony would be held in about thirty minutes and she had enough time to wash off the top layer of dirt and get something to drink before she was needed on the podium.

She didn't think Frank would be in the trailer and breathed a sigh of relief when he wasn't. He was probably jockeying for position behind the cameras wearing his traditional TKS shirt and ball cap. What a media whore, she thought, gulping a bottle of berry-flavored Gatorade.

Twenty minutes later the crowd was still thick around Caroline. Shannon recognized many of the well-wishers as other riders who had not fared so well this round but could very easily be in her shoes the next. Shannon froze when she spotted the man standing next to Caroline. She had seen Steven Davis at several events, but she'd never ventured this close to him since the day he threw her out of Caroline's room. She wanted to talk to Caroline more than she wanted to avoid her father.

He wasn't as imposing or frightening as she remembered, but then again she had thought he was going to kill her—or at least beat the crap out of her. His hair was more salt than pepper, his stomach carrying an extra ten pounds, but the smile on his face as he looked at his daughter said it all.

Shannon often wondered what happened between Caroline and her father after she was unceremoniously tossed. From the way they were hugging, it was evident that their relationship had not suffered any ill effects from that moment.

The woman standing on the other side of Caroline could be none other than her mother. The resemblance was remarkable, and Shannon knew exactly what Caroline would look like in another thirty or so years. She would be a beautiful woman.

Shannon approached Caroline and her family not sure what to expect. She wanted to congratulate her and it was now or never. She gathered up her nerve and stepped forward. Good grief, she thought, that episode was water under the bridge. He probably didn't even remember her. Yeah, and Christmas never fell on December twenty-fifth.

Shannon kept her eyes on Davis as she approached. She knew the second he saw her and the instant he recognized her. Confusion, shock, disbelief, and then finally anger settled onto his face. There was no backing out now. She was no longer that frightened seventeen-year-old girl.

"Congratulations, Caroline," she said stepping into their circle. She held out her hand and it appeared that Caroline took it more out of habit from the dozens of times today than realizing it was from Shannon.

Caroline's hand was warm, the rough edges of blisters and calluses tickling Shannon's hand. A bolt of something shot up her arm, down her throat, and settled in her midsection. Caroline's expression changed from exuberant to pleasant.

"Thank you."

"Your ride was great. One down, ten to go," Shannon added referring to the remaining races in the championship.

"I just focus on one at a time." Caroline looked between Shannon and her father and fear and uncertainty clouded her eyes. It was obvious that she didn't know what to do with the two of them standing so close to each other.

"Mr. Davis, I'm Shannon Roberts." Shannon thought it would be stupid to add, "I'm sure you remember me," or "I was a friend of your daughter's in high school," or better yet, "I'm the one you caught with her hand down your daughter's shorts." She extended her hand.

Davis paused before taking it and shaking it firmly. "Yes, I remember." He hesitated again as if deciding to be polite or kick her butt. "Excellent ride this weekend."

Shannon thought the entire world could hear her sigh of relief. "Thank you, sir, but Caroline was better. You must be very proud of her."

Davis visibly relaxed a bit. "Yes, we are. We've always been proud of her." Shannon noticed he didn't add "no matter what" to the end of his statement.

Shannon started to back away. "Well, I don't mean to intrude. I just wanted to congratulate you, Caroline. See you in Mount Anne." Shannon turned and almost ran into a photographer snapping pictures of them together. She knew that photo would be in a magazine or newspaper before too long. The headline would probably read RIVALS BURYING THE HATCHET. If it were only true.

Caroline watched Shannon walk away and only then began to breathe again. When she realized that her father had recognized Shannon immediately, she felt like a deer caught in the headlights. She didn't know whether to introduce them or say, "Dad, you remember Shannon." What if he didn't? Then what? How would she follow up with that one? Shit, this was awkward.

"Who was that, darling?"

Her mother's voice pierced through her confusion and Caroline shot a questioning look at her father. As far as she knew, he had never told her mother what he walked in on that day. After Shannon had left her room she expected him to shout or scream at her, maybe even yank her out of school. But he did none of those.

Steven Davis was a calm man and that was what scared Caroline the most after the door closed behind Shannon. Dean Phillips started to apologize, but he silenced her with a look and a shake of his head, effectively dismissing her. Caroline wanted nothing more than to disappear between the seams in the plush carpet. She was humiliated, mortified. She knew this was the time to keep her mouth shut. At least until he cooled off. After several minutes of pacing back and forth in the small room he finally spoke.

"How long has this been going on?" His voice was terrifyingly quiet.

"We met last summer." She smartly left out the part about how they had met.

"I see. Who approached who?"

Caroline knew he was asking if she was lured into what he had just witnessed.

"I did," Caroline said. It was a small white lie because she had noticed Shannon well before Shannon noticed her.

"I see," he repeated.

"Daddy—" she said. He held up his hand and stopped her from continuing.

"I'm asking the questions here," he said. "Is she the first...the only..." He struggled to find the right words.

Caroline knew what he was getting at. Was this a phase, an experiment, or the real thing? She risked his ire trying to ease his misery.

"I've suspected for a long time. I've always been more interested in my *girl* friends than boys. *I* did this, Dad, not the other way around. I knew what I was doing." The *this* she was referring to was deciding to accept she was a lesbian versus being lured or forced into it.

"I see," he said for the third time. It was what he always said when he didn't know what to say.

"Do you, Dad? I'm sorry this is how you had to find out. I never meant it to be like this. I was going to tell you and Mom in a few years once I was away from here. I didn't want you thinking I became a lesbian because of MHA." He cringed when she said the word "lesbian." She stepped closer to him.

"Daddy, I know how much you sacrificed so that I could come here. This is a great place, for a school of course. But MHA did not make me a lesbian. Being around girls all the time does not make you a lesbian any more than being on a football team makes you gay. I have always been this way. MHA just gave me the confidence to be who I am. To take charge of my life. To be responsible for my actions. That's who I've become. I'm still your daughter and I love you, Daddy, regardless of who I'm attracted to."

He lowered his head and Caroline didn't know if he was corralling his anger or getting ready to release it. Her knees were shaking and she felt like she needed to throw up. Finally, after several agonizing minutes, he turned to her.

"This afternoon will remain between you and me. If you decide this is the way you want to live your life you can tell me and your mother together. I'll act appropriately surprised and we'll go from there."

"But where do *we* go from here, Daddy?" Caroline had a special relationship with her father, one that she knew had drastically changed the minute he walked into her room.

"You were partially right, Caroline. MHA gave you the confidence to be who you are. To take charge of your life. To be responsible for your actions. That's who you are, but your mother and I played a part in it as well. You are my daughter, no matter what, and I will always love you, but I'd be lying if I said I know what to do. Give me time, Caroline, and I ask that you give your mother time when you tell her. This has come as quite a shock, as you can imagine, and it will take time to process."

It had taken time for her parents to recover from the shock but once they did, they were fully supportive of her. It was even more evident that they were by her side now, at the finish of her major comeback race. Her mother repeated her question. "Someone I knew at MHA." Her mother had never met Shannon while they were both students at MHA and as far as Caroline knew, she still knew nothing about the circumstances when her father had met Shannon.

"What a coincidence, and she's a rider too. That's wonderful, Caroline. Someone you can reminisce with. You two have so much in common."

Caroline exchanged glances with her father. Her mother was sometimes absolutely clueless.

Chapter Eight

"C D!" Caroline heard the familiar voice before she saw the owner. Searching the crowd passing through the door from customs, Caroline finally saw a hand waving frantically in the air. Attached to it was Fran.

She jostled through the people waiting for their arrivals and was quickly enveloped in a bear hug that practically squeezed the breath out of her.

"Good grief, Fran. It's not like you haven't seen me in years." Caroline pried herself out of her grasp. "It's only been a week."

"Sure, but we're on a totally different continent." That was Fran's way of thinking and Caroline understood it perfectly. Fran was staying with Caroline and would be able to watch the second stage of the championships. That is, if Caroline made it that far.

Having flown into Inverness, they had an hour-long drive to Mount Anne, one of the largest towns in the highlands of Scotland, for the second race. They chatted nonstop from the airport to Caroline's hotel, and by the time Fran's luggage was out of the car, they had caught up on just about everything.

It was just after noon and having slept on the plane, Fran was ready to see the sights. Caroline had arrived four days earlier and was settled into the routine, the time zone, and the food. They strolled through the main shopping area in Mount Anne before returning to the hotel and crashing in the lounge.

After their drinks were served and their appetizers devoured Fran said, "So tell me about the race." Next to her parents and siblings, Fran was her biggest fan.

"Well, the World Cup is the biggest mountain bike event in Scotland. The course is about three miles long and is one of the most difficult terrains in the series. It draws about twenty-five thousand spectators and ten times that many watch it on TV."

"Ooo, you'd better look good, girl," Fran said poking her in the side. "No, wait, you're the one that's camera shy; it's Shannon Roberts that always looks good on camera."

Caroline had been trying to forget Shannon was in the same small town this week, but having already seen her several times walking around on the event grounds, she had finally given up.

"I'll bet she looks better from any angle." Fran raised her eyebrows.

"Is there something you need to tell me, Fran?"

"What? Oh God no. Sorry, no offense."

"None taken."

"It's just that she's a knockout. Anyone with two eyes can see that. She sits on your side of the bench. I'm surprised you haven't said anything about her."

The shift in the conversation to Shannon made Caroline uncomfortable. "What do you mean?"

"Come on, Caroline, you might be out of practice, but you certainly aren't dead. You must have noticed how she fills out those spandex shorts."

"They're Lycra."

"Lycra, spandex, Saran Wrap, who cares? Well, the Saran Wrap might be interesting. Anyway, the point is that there is nothing left to the imagination when she's wearing those, except what she tastes like."

"Fran!" Caroline choked on her cocktail, drawing the attention of several patrons in the lounge.

"Don't Fran me, Caroline. I know damn good and well you lezzies talk about girls the same way guys do and the same way we straight chicks talk about guys. Don't look at me that way."

Caroline wasn't sure just how she was looking at Fran.

"How many riders on the circuit are queer?" Fran only used the term in the most affectionate way.

"How should I know? I don't go around and ask to see their sexual orientation card." Caroline signaled the waiter for another drink.

"Jeez, CD, I've been hanging around you long enough that even I can tell who's queer and who's not. And Shannon Roberts is definitely one of yours."

"She was once." Caroline let her statement hang in the air like a berry ripe for the picking.

"What? When? How long? Was she as good as she looks?" She rattled off questions in rapid fire.

"Yep, in high school, about ten months, and absolutely."

"Holy shit, tell me more. Tell me everything, and I mean *every*thing." Fran was sitting on the edge of her chair in anticipation.

She and Fran hung out together as much as their schedules allowed, shared practically everything with each other including celebrating new love and wiping the tears of old love. But Caroline had never told her about Shannon. The memories were too painful. But after seeing Shannon again, talking to her, Caroline needed someone to help her sort it all out.

She relayed the story from the first time she saw Shannon in freshman English, to the first time they had sex. Funny how she didn't consider it making love. They were teenagers, and teenagers didn't make love, they had sex. And lots of it. She ended with the scene in her dorm room.

"Holy shit," Fran so eloquently summarized, collapsing back in her chair.

"I'll say." Caroline filled her in on her meeting Shannon at their first race.

"And you haven't spoken to her in all that time until last week in Canada?"

"No. It's a small circuit and we'd see each other at practically every race, but she kept her distance and I kept mine."

"So what happened in Canada?"

That was the question Caroline kept asking herself. What had made Shannon finally say something to her? "I don't know. She came out of nowhere straight toward me. She had to track me down. It wasn't as if we literally ran into each other in the ladies room. She just started talking to me and then when she congratulated me when my father was standing next to me, I thought I was going to die."

"Double holy shit."

"And we're in the same hotel." Caroline held up her hand. "Don't say it."

"I don't know what to say. First you tell me you had sex with the hottest thing in bike shorts, then you tell me your father caught you in the act, then she speaks to you for the first time in almost ten years, and now she's in your hotel. Have I got all that right?"

"That's about it."

"Are you sure? You're not going to tell me you have a love child you've kept hidden away all these years are you? I don't think my heart or my clit can take any more."

They both laughed, releasing some of the tension in Caroline's stomach. "No, the love child is safely tucked away for a few more years."

"What are you going to do?"

"About what?" Caroline asked.

"About Shannon."

"What about her?"

Fran sighed. "Did you hit your head on your last ride or something? Are you going to try to find out what's gotten into her...so to speak?" She winked at Caroline.

"There's nothing to do. She's here to try to win the championship, just like I am."

"Bullshit. You two have some unfinished business you need to iron out."

Caroline was getting frustrated. "It was ten years ago. Let it go. I have."

Fran laid her hand over Caroline's. "It doesn't matter how long it's been. The circumstance around the way she walked away from you is a big deal."

Caroline signaled for the bill and used the action to end the conversation and get her thoughts together. Was Fran right? Did they have unfinished business? Why did she never hear from Shannon? Why did she finally talk to her after all this time? And did she have the guts to get the answers to those questions?

Chapter Nine

The Downhill is a high-speed descent down the Nevis Range course—a grueling, rock-strewn ribbon of bike-smashing dirt that drops five hundred twenty-five meters in two point seven kilometers. It's rider against the clock. And the mountain," Fran recited behind her.

"What are you talking about?"

Fran waved a piece of paper at her. "The information about the race. I printed it off the Web. It says right here that the current course record is four minutes and forty-three seconds held by none other than your Shannon Roberts."

"She's not my anything," Caroline said but was ignored.

"And just how far is five hundred twenty-five meters and two point seven kilometers? When is the U.S. going to get in line with the rest of the world and start using metric?"

Caroline shook her head and smiled at her. "Which answer do you want first? The one that is 'seventeen hundred feet in a mile and a half,' or the phrase 'not in our lifetime'?" They were getting ready to go out to dinner and Caroline was just getting out of the shower.

"How do you like being one of the people competing at the highest level? 'Famous names, heroes from the magazines, Olympic and world champions will be here as they compete for important world championship points,'" Fran read as she turned the page.

"Pretty damn important, so that means you get to buy dinner. Now get out of here so I can get dressed." Caroline stuck her tongue out at her and slammed the bathroom door.

An hour later they sat at a table enjoying a glass of wine. The restaurant was crowded, but they chose a table outside to enjoy the evening and watch the people walk by.

"When do you defend?" Fran asked about her dissertation. Fran had been her proofreader and knew almost every word of her thesis. Caroline knew she had no idea what she was reading but wanted to help just the same.

"Three weeks after I get back." The critical date loomed over her and would until it was over.

"How do you do this and study at the same time?" Fran waved her hand at the other racers.

"If I don't know it by now, I don't deserve to get my Ph.D. Supernova-driven interstellar turbulence is not something you cram for in a few days."

"True," Fran said. "Here, you've got to taste this." She stabbed a piece of pasta and extended her fork across the table. Caroline took the bite, but before she could comment on the spicy taste Fran said, "There she is."

"Who?" Caroline knew the answer to the question but asked it anyway.

"Who, hell? Shannon Roberts and she is coming this way. No, don't look…"

"I wasn't going to. I know what she looks like and I don't care where she is." Then why is my heart racing and my throat all of a sudden very dry?

"Bullshit. Oh man, she is hotter in real life than in her pictures. She's looking this way, she's—"

Caroline set her drink on the table a little harder than she intended. The wine spilled over the edge of the glass. "I don't want a play-by-play commentary of her evening, Fran." By the look on Fran's face, she was up to something. When she motioned to Shannon to come to the table, Caroline knew she wasn't going to like it.

"Too bad; here she comes." Caroline took a deep breath in anticipation of seeing those piercing blue eyes again.

"Caroline? I don't want to interrupt, but I wanted to congratulate you again and wish you luck this week."

Shannon was standing, and since Caroline was still seated she had to look up past a pair of memorable breasts to meet her eyes. The dryness in her throat rapidly progressed to her mouth.

"Thank you. The same to you," she babbled. Fran nudged her under the table and she remembered her manners. "Shannon Roberts, Fran Loming," she said by way of introduction.

"Pleased to meet you, Shannon. I've heard so much about you," Fran said sweetly.

It was Caroline's turn to kick her under the table. Shannon's eyes narrowed as she gave Fran more than a cursory once-over. She didn't look happy.

"Thank you, Fran was it?" Shannon asked.

"Yes. Even though I'm a very big Caroline Davis fan, good luck to you as well."

Caroline could have sworn her very straight friend was flirting with Shannon but knew it had to be her imagination. Shannon focused her attention back on her.

"I won't keep you, Caroline. Have a nice evening."

"Wow." Fran sighed to Shannon's back as she walked away. "She is so hot she sizzles. My God, Caroline, was she always like that? She practically left burn marks in the floor. Every woman was looking at her and a few are going after her."

Caroline had not yet begun to breathe normally again, and Fran's chatter about Shannon's sexual magnetism didn't help her scattered nerves.

"If anyone could make me turn the corner, it would be her."

"Stop it," Caroline snapped. Fran looked shocked at her outburst.

Caroline softened her voice. "I'm sorry. I didn't mean to bark at you. It's just that this race is…the series…"

"Bullshit," Fran said again. She had such a way with the English language. "There is something going on between you two, and the sooner you admit it and do something about it the better off you'll be. Jesus, the way she looked at me, I thought she was going to knock me out of my chair and wipe the floor with me."

"Fran, please." She didn't want to get into it again with her today. Fran was relentless, and she was just not up to it.

Shannon had walked out on her once and she had said nothing more than polite conversation until a week ago. She thought they had something special going on, but obviously it was just a high school fling. They had to jump through all kinds of hoops to finally talk to each other after her father caught them, but it had never been the same. Their conversations were forced and as much as she willed it, their connection was lost.

"Okay, CD," Fran said. "I'll leave it alone. At least for now. You've got to concentrate or you'll fall down the two point seven meter mountain and break your freakin' neck. Then I'd really have to spoon feed you."

Caroline forced a laugh and couldn't wait until the check came.

❖

Shannon paced her room, oblivious to the food on the room service tray getting cold. She had gone to Ms. Farren's for a quick bite to eat prior to venturing out to enjoy the sights, sounds, and beauties of the Scottish countryside.

She'd been keyed up lately, snapping at everyone and drinking way too much. Other times when she got like this she simply needed to blow off some steam in the arms of a woman on the dance floor and the bedroom floor. Or the living room floor, or the foyer floor, or any number of other hard surfaces that were handy.

Seeing Caroline and her date enjoying a romantic, chummy dinner was not what she needed tonight. She should have turned and walked right back out the door but instead found herself standing beside their table. Caroline and *Fran*. The name gave her a sour taste in her mouth. They were obviously close. Body language said volumes more than words, and they definitely had spent more than superficial time together.

It felt like a fist hit her stomach as she imagined Fran touching Caroline, kissing her, stroking her to orgasm. She had no right to feel possessive about a woman she didn't really know anymore. She had no right to her. Hell, she gave up that right ten years ago when she threw her under the bus that just so happened to have her father at the wheel and Dean Phillips in the co-pilot seat.

She had no idea why she still felt something for Caroline. Sure, she was drop-dead gorgeous, but so were the dozens of women she had slept with, and she barely remembered some of them. Maybe it was because of the way they had ended things. For years, she had dreams about Caroline. They were set in the places where they used to go together—the movies, the local diner, the back corner of the library. But mixed in were current places and people she knew. Caroline was happy, sad, furious, and teasing all in the same dream. Shannon felt like she was sneaking to or away from something and she had just gotten caught with her hand in the cookie jar. She didn't need Freud to tell her what that meant. More often than not, her dreams didn't make any sense and she woke feeling tired and disjointed because she had spent the entire night trying to figure out what in the hell was going on.

Shannon grabbed her jacket, her wallet, and room key and closed the door firmly behind her. She needed to get out and do something. Anything to get her mind off Caroline. Caroline was a sexy, sensuous woman and there was no doubt in her mind what she and *Fran* were probably doing now.

"Fran, what kind of stupid nineteen forties name is that?" she asked the empty hall. "Francis? Francine? Francesca?" She tried the names out while waiting for the elevator.

Losing patience, she strode to the door marked *Stairs* and bounded them two at a time to the first floor. She had no specific destination in mind, but after exiting the revolving door she turned right and headed toward the bright lights of the expo area of the race. Workers were still setting up booths, tents, and vendor displays, so the place was lit up like midday. Shannon wandered around the grounds tripping twice and almost falling on some stray cable and electrical cords. She'd better be careful, she told herself. With her luck, tonight she'd trip, fall, and break her arm over some stupid orange cord no bigger around than a thick pencil.

"Shannon?" A vaguely familiar voice came from her left. "Shannon, I thought that was you. I knew you were going to be here this week. I was hoping we'd run into each other again."

As the woman rambled Shannon finally recognized her. Gail. She couldn't think of her last name, if she even knew it in the first place, but she did remember the night she had spent with the tall blonde.

"Gail, how have you been?" Shannon asked hoping she'd gotten the name right.

"Fine, but I'm much better now that you're here." She stepped closer, and Shannon saw Gail's eyes drift over her body. The simmer reflecting back at her told Shannon that Gail knew what lay beneath her shorts and TKS emblazoned T-shirt.

Shannon's body remembered Gail. Her pulse began to beat a little faster and that familiar tingle in her groin told her she was more than ready for some fun. It had been several weeks since the last time she had been with someone and that was about the maximum she could go without feeling edgy and cranky.

Maybe that was her problem with Caroline. The memories of her and Caroline together were igniting an already smoldering itch. Her body was craving attention and slamming into her past was like throwing fuel on a fire.

This had to stop. She had to quit thinking about Caroline, what they had and what it was like. It was over, done, history. This was the here and now. Caroline was after her trophy. Her spot atop the mountain.

Shannon had never really been all that competitive; her skill on the bike came naturally. If she put her mind to it, she would win and win big, but if not, she was okay with a second or an occasional third place finish. She had money of her own thanks to her lucrative endorsements. She owned her home in Denver and her cabin in Big Bear free and clear. She had several cars in her garage and the world at her fingertips.

She had no burning need to win the championship; it was just what she did—win races. She didn't need to prove something to herself or anyone else. She knew how good she was and so did the rest of the mountain biking world.

Her fan base followed her around the globe. Where they got their money to hang out with a bunch of gear heads she had no idea, and frankly, didn't care. They talked bikes, gear ratios, and with very little encouragement she could get them to talk dirty in her ear in the middle of the night.

"Shannon?"

The sound of her name brought her back to her present surroundings. Gail was standing right in front of her, and while Shannon took a stroll down memory lane, Gail had moved closer.

"Sorry, what did you say?"

Gail winked at her and leaned in. "I asked if you wanted to hook up again. I remember having a mind-bending good time."

Gail was so close her breath tickled Shannon's ear. She didn't have to whisper; there was no one within twenty yards of them. An involuntary shudder ran down Shannon's spine when Caroline's face popped into her brain.

"Sure, why not? Let's go." Shannon grabbed Gail's hand and pulled her toward the nearest dark corner. She had had it with Caroline Davis messing with her mind. She was rich, famous, and young. There was plenty of life to live and she'd be goddamned if she would continue to have her panties in a bunch over one woman. There were dozens, if not three times that many, for her to choose from. If any woman didn't want her, then she didn't want her. With Gail giggling loudly, Shannon stepped behind a delivery truck.

CHAPTER TEN

The next three days were a blur of photo ops, sponsor commitments, and practice runs. By the end of each day, Caroline was exhausted. The added stress of actually trying to win the race almost seemed secondary, but the reality was overwhelming.

Caroline had competed at this level for several years and one race was basically the same as the next. What made this race so special was the one before and the nine after. It wasn't just one race that made the difference, even though one race could be the difference between standing on the top box of the winner's stand and standing on the second or third box.

The world championship was the one thing Caroline wanted. What she had worked for. Sure, she had gone to school for what seemed like forever and all she had left was to spend three hours defending her thesis and she'd be able to put Ph.D. behind her name. But this was hers. No one could help her with this. Not her parents, who had packed up their travel trailer and cheered her on at every race in the country and most outside as well. Fran was her best friend, but all she could do was offer words of encouragement and change her bandages when she was injured. Her sponsors provided her the tools to win, but only she could do it.

The night before the first qualifying heats, Caroline was restless, too restless to sit in her room. Fran had tried to interest her in a game of cards or a movie on the hotel pay-per-view movie channel, even going so far as to suggest they watch a porn movie and have a private moment with themselves under the sheets.

"Are you nuts!" was Caroline's response to that one. "I have to sit on a saddle as wide as pencil lead, barrel down a mountain at thirty miles an hour with nothing between me and Mother Earth, and you want me to fuck myself?"

"I just thought it would relax you. You've been so uptight the last few days."

"I've been uptight because I have a race to win. A very big race." Caroline emphasized the last few words. "I can't race with my legs feeling like over-cooked spaghetti noodles and my clit so sensitive I can't even walk. What are you thinking? Are you intentionally trying to sabotage me?"

Fran held up her hands in surrender. "Okay, okay. So maybe this isn't a good time for a little one-on-one. I've never seen you so nervous. Yes, I know this is a very big race," Fran repeated Caroline's description, "but you never let these things get to you."

Fran was right. Caroline was rarely nervous about much of anything. She always came fully prepared no matter if it were a mid-term, a job interview, or a race. If she hadn't mastered it by now, there was nothing left to do.

Caroline knew what it was. Shannon was getting to her. Hell, Shannon had gotten to her the minute their eyes finally met after all these years. She was her nemesis on the mountain, her competitor for the championship, and the first girl she had freely given her heart to.

She had been able to maintain distance, both physically and emotionally, from Shannon for years. The only time she really thought about her was at these races. They crossed paths and occasionally stood beside each other on the winner's stand, but had never said anything more than a casual hello. So why now?

"Let's go for a walk," Caroline said.

Fran glanced at the clock. "Now it's your turn to be nuts. It's after ten."

"Come on; who cares? You're my best friend, and as such, in charge of my emotional well-being. Since you think I need a distraction it's your responsibility to come with me." To Caroline it was as simple as that.

Fran grumbled something Caroline couldn't decipher and was still squawking when they stepped out of the elevator. The lobby was busy with several people at the front desk, another three or four sitting on the couches by the unlit fireplace. Loud voices drifted from the bar area. Not everyone was tucked tightly into bed at this hour.

Caroline saw Shannon first. She frowned at the disheveled look she had acquired. Her hair looked like her hands had been in it all evening. Her clothes were askew and was that road rash on her knee? She frowned but changed her expression and disposition, and as Shannon walked toward them, she felt the heat rise in her chest. There, right there on her neck, just above her collar, was a hickey. An honest to God, high school hickey.

"Speaking of getting fucked," Caroline said under her breath loud enough for Fran to hear. When Shannon looked at her with fire in her eyes, Caroline realized her comment carried much farther than she intended.

"When in Rome," Shannon said sarcastically as she passed by Caroline and Fran and punched the elevator button.

Caroline knew Shannon was staying at the same hotel and wasn't surprised to see her in the lobby. The sponsor of the championship had reserved a block of rooms for the riders and Caroline had taken advantage of the cheaper rates this time.

"What was that all about?" Fran asked watching Shannon walk away.

"How the hell would I know? I'm not her keeper," Caroline barked. A pang of red-hot jealousy burned in her gut and she was furious at herself for letting Shannon ignite it again.

"Don't snap at me," Fran said. "I just asked a simple question. And speaking of simple questions, was that a hickey I saw on her neck? I haven't seen one of those in years."

"Shut up, Fran." Caroline practically marched across the lobby and out the door Shannon had recently come through.

"For someone who says there's nothing going on, you sure aren't acting like it."

"I said shut up, Fran."

"I saw the look in your eye. You wanted to throttle her."

Caroline stopped so quickly it took Fran several steps before she realized she was walking alone. Caroline was hot all over and she knew her face must be beet red. "I told you. Shannon Roberts is old news. Very old news. The only thing we have in common anymore is trying to win this championship. She can fuck whomever she wants. It's none of my business and I don't care if her entire body is covered with hickeys." At one time it had been, and Caroline was the one who had put them there.

It was a long weekend in early November when Caroline's roommate had gone home for a family wedding. The minute class was over on Friday afternoon Shannon was at her door. They didn't leave her room the entire three days except for an occasional trip to the cafeteria to be seen and to replenish their tired bodies.

Caroline had dared Shannon to let her give her a hickey and when she finally agreed, one thing led to another and after another marathon round of kissing, sucking, touching, and licking, Shannon had dozens of hickeys that stretched from the top of her thighs to just below her collarbone.

They laughed about it at the time like seventeen-year-olds would, but when Shannon had to change her clothes in the locker room for tennis class it wasn't so funny after all. Before the end of the day, Shannon's body was the topic of conversation. Several of the girls knew she and Shannon were friends and asked her about it. At first Caroline was mortified, but after a while she considered it her mark and she was damn proud of it. Shannon's reputation as a bad girl was reinforced after that weekend.

No longer in the mood for a walk, but knowing she couldn't go back into the hotel, at least not yet, Caroline walked.

"Hey, CD, slow down." Fran caught up with her. "I sit behind a desk all day. Give me a break, will ya? I didn't mean to piss you off."

"You didn't," Caroline replied truthfully. Shannon did by saying hello to her in Canada, and the very fresh bite mark on her neck said even more.

CHAPTER ELEVEN

Shannon was third out of the chute the afternoon of the first day of qualifying. Hundreds of riders and fans had come to Ben Nevis on the slopes of Aonach Mor the last week in June. Mount Anne was the closest town and the second race in the championship series was named after it.

Forty riders had descended the trail ahead of her, one starting every five minutes. In the last two days she had ridden the course several times and had memorized every twist and turn on the difficult trail. This morning as she eyed the leader board, several riders had crossed the finish line bleeding, one severely from her knee. It was obvious to everyone nasty spills were still an everyday event at the championships. Every rider was giving it her all and pulled out all the stops to win.

The bell rang and Shannon shot off the starting line. The course immediately dropped fifteen feet and Shannon was pedaling before her rear tire hit the rock-strewn ground. Her left arm came perilously close to a tree branch, but she barely noticed, her concentration on two places, the ground directly in front of her and what lay ahead.

She had on all her safety gear. Her arms were covered by the long sleeves of her shirt, courtesy of TKS and her other sponsors, her chest protector underneath. Her bright green gloves were cinched tight and didn't move as she squeezed her brakes at just the right time to slide into the next turn. She had worn her helmet and goggles so many times they felt like they weren't even there. It had been difficult to adjust to the full-face helmet after riding for so many years with just a simple brain bucket, as they were known, but for her own safety she had switched. When she first got it she wore it everywhere around her house, even when she mowed the lawn and repaired her bike. It was now as much a part of her as her own hands and she felt naked every time she was on her bike without it. It had probably saved her life more than once too.

Leaning over the handlebars, she pushed her right leg down and pulled her left leg up, shifting gears to climb the steep grade. This part of the course had the steepest incline and she was breathing hard. Focusing on each pedal stroke, she arrived at the peak. There was no time to stop and admire the scenery, some of Scotland's best, because she was determined to come down the mountain the fastest.

No wider than the width of handlebars, the final section was where the race separated the big girls from the little girls. She nicked a bush with her elbow and an even bigger one with her right leg. She felt and heard nothing but her raspy breathing inside the helmet. One more turn and she would be on the straightaway to cross the finish line.

She hit the turn with every skill she had, alternately braking and accelerating so as not to slide in the loose dirt. On her last practice run, this was where she had dumped it, and as she got up she noticed that several others had as well. Dried blood covered several rocks.

Out of the last turn, she finally heard the noise of the crowd. They were five and six deep, screaming, shouting, and blowing air horns as she rode under the black and white sign. Shannon skidded to a showy stop and looked to the board for her time.

"Damn," she said. She was two seconds slower than her own course record time. What had happened? She thought she had a pretty clean ride, except for the fourth turn, that was a bit sloppy. She took off her helmet and pedaled out of the finish area; another rider would arrive in a few minutes.

"Shannon, you're bleeding."

Shannon looked and for the first time noticed blood dripping down her leg. It was flowing pretty freely and her sock had turned from white to red. A drop hit the dirt as she looked at it.

"You'd better get that looked at, honey."

Shannon found the voice of the endearment and Gail was looking at her with concern written on her face.

"Thanks, I will," she replied, quickly pedaling away from the woman she had taken behind the trailer two nights ago. If she tagged along, it would mean there was something more between them than two people sharing a quickie. She had no intention of letting Gail get that impression.

❖

Her destination wasn't the med tent but the JumboTron where she could watch Caroline's ride down the mountain. By the time she got there Caroline was crossing the finish line ahead of Shannon, three tenths of a second faster than her. Shannon would be going into the finals tomorrow in second place.

Forty-five minutes and twelve stitches later, Shannon limped to the TKS trailer. Greg Mitchell, Frank's number one goon and gopher, was standing by the door as if guarding against an invasion. This was a bike race, not the World Cup where sailboat owners kept their keels hidden behind screens so their competitors couldn't see how their boats were designed. How ridiculous.

Bike racing was as transparent as it got. Everyone knew who rode what bike, the frame composition, the stem length, the crank shaft, gear ratio, front fork rise, and tires. It was open knowledge, but nobody copied each other in an attempt to win. At this level, no two bikes were the same because it was the rider that made them different.

Her bike was a TKS Road Rage with a custom made carbon head tube for precise steering, Shimano disc brakes tuned to her specs, Shimano XTR components, and a one-of-a-kind crankset. Her tires were Kenda Nevegal inflated to 28 psi, and her forks had four-inch travel.

"Watch my bike," she said to the goon. She never left her bike unattended, but Mitchell knew her and his place in her life and would make sure it didn't ride away.

"What the hell happened?" Frank barked before she stepped her second foot inside. "You're off by two seconds and Davis is ahead of you."

She forced herself not to hobble to the nearest chair. She practically collapsed into it and put her leg up on an adjacent chair. "Nothing, Frank. For Christ sake, it's only the qualifying ride, not the end of the world. I could ride that mountain with my eyes closed if I had enough time. Tomorrow is when it matters, so get off my back."

Shannon was uncharacteristically short with her sponsor and by the look on his face, he was not too pleased. She backpedaled. "Look, Frank, I'll win the race tomorrow. If not, there's France and Madrid." She began pulling off her shirt. She wore an undershirt beneath her chest protector. The pressure suit was injection molded to fit her body and offered the ultimate in upper body protection. With injection molded plastic cups on the shoulder, arms, and forearms, and the high impact breast plate and thumb loops to keep it in place, Shannon always thought she looked like a storm trooper in *Star Wars*.

"Relax, Frank. TKS is getting plenty of face time and you'll make buckets of money. Stop worrying and enjoy it." What she wanted to say was stop acting like a spoiled little boy who had to win every race. He wasn't even riding, the fat bastard. Shannon had never even seen him on a bike. Other owners and designers took their creations for a spin once in a while, if not to evaluate the design, then for the sheer enjoyment of biking.

"Now if you don't mind, I'd like to get changed," Shannon said, effectively dismissing her paycheck.

Finally alone, Shannon sat and surveyed the damage to her leg. The stitches had closed the cut, and by the throbbing in her calf, the lidocaine was starting to wear off. She looked around the trailer. The contents were comfortably familiar. She knew more about bikes and components than most of the mechanics. She could probably disassemble and reassemble her bike blindfolded. There were many days she felt more comfortable with her bike than with people.

She was good with small talk. She knew what she had to say to whom, and who to shake hands with. She easily chatted up the sponsors and did all the things society expected her to do, but she rarely related to people on a purely personal level. She went through the motions, said the right things, and did what was required of her, but if anyone in her immediate circle were to disappear or even die, she doubted she would even miss them. The people in her life were superficial and lasted as long as her last win. Pulling on her shorts, she heard the door latch click behind her.

"What a magnificent sight."

Shannon froze when she heard the voice. Half dressed was not the position she wanted to be in with Nikki Striker. She pulled her shirt on over her bare chest, giving herself a few moments to get herself together.

The wife of her major sponsor had been coming on to her for months. Nikki believed you could never be too rich, too thin, or too forward. Her husband made her the first, starving took care of the second, and she took care of the last all by herself.

It was during the U.S. National Championship series when she had made her first move. Actually, she had probably been coming on to her since her husband signed Shannon, but Shannon was too caught up in her own life to notice. When she finally did, she didn't know whether to run or take Nikki up on her offer. Nikki became increasingly aggressive until one night she caught Shannon alone in a trailer very similar to the one they were in now.

"Hey, baby," Nikki had said in a sexy voice. Even though she was on the thin side of Shannon's tastes, Nikki was five foot five, had a perfect pair of manufactured breasts, long legs, and volumes of billowy black hair.

"Frank left about five minutes ago. You can probably catch him at the media tent." She bent and tied her shoes and when she straightened, Nikki was directly in front of her.

"I'm not looking for Frank." The way she came on to Shannon, Nikki was definitely not interested in her husband or his dick. She was the trophy wife with Frank at least twenty-five years her senior.

Shannon knew she was playing with fire but asked anyway. "What are you looking for, Nikki?" Nikki stepped even closer, her eyes bright with what Shannon recognized as lust. Her stomach skirted into her throat. She had to be very careful. If she played this wrong, she could be in big trouble, the least of which was losing her sponsor. No matter her popularity in the series, without a main sponsor it would be difficult but not impossible to continue racing.

Nikki ran a perfectly manicured finger down the center of her chest, pausing between her breasts before tracing the TKS letters on her T-shirt. "I'm looking for fun. And I think you're just the one who can give it to me."

Shannon wanted to knock the spindly hand away but clenched her fist to her side instead. "Really?"

"Yes, really," Nikki answered. Her breath smelled like a wintergreen Tic Tac, her perfume Chanel.

"What makes you think that?" Shannon asked, feeling cocky. Maybe she could just tease her along for the next few races and then she'd be out of her hair.

"Your reputation precedes you." Shannon could practically feel the lust pouring out of Nikki's body. "Rumor has it you're discreet and very, very good. Leaving the girls begging for more."

Shannon inched back just enough to give her some breathing room but not so much that Nikki would notice. She had to maintain the upper hand in this conversation. "You don't believe everything you hear, do you?"

That made Nikki laugh. A throaty laugh that could have been mistaken for a heavy smoker's cough. "I do when it comes to you. As a matter of fact," Nikki's eyes roamed Shannon's body as if imagining what she looked like under her husband's clothing line, "I'd like to come for you."

"What would your husband say?" Shannon asked, planning her escape around Nikki if she needed one. "Or does he want to watch?" The thought sickened her.

Nikki laughed again and this time Shannon's stomach reeled.

"Oh, I'd bet he'd like to, but this is my private party. It's by invitation only and his must have gotten lost in the mail." She licked her lips.

Shannon was suddenly tired of the game and smoothly stepped around Nikki, leaving her standing facing the wall. "I don't think that would be a good idea."

It wasn't long before Nikki spun around, the lust in her eyes replaced with anger. Her voice was not as calm as it had been a moment earlier. "And why not? No one needs to know, especially Frank. It'll be our little secret."

"I'm not good at keeping secrets, and I don't fuck where I bank, so to speak," she added cautiously. "I don't mean to offend you, and I'm flattered, but I don't do married women and I certainly don't do the boss's wife." Okay, one white lie was acceptable given the circumstances.

Nikki had surprised her by accepting the rejection graciously and she had stayed away from Shannon until now. "Nikki, I didn't think you came to races on the other side of the pond."

"I thought a change of scenery would be good for me. You know, new city, new terrain, old friends."

"And what do you think of Scotland?" Shannon asked moving so that her back was not against a wall. The last thing she needed was for Nikki to pin her against it and lay a big fat sloppy wet one on her.

"Gorgeous," she replied. Nikki moved between Shannon and the door.

"I didn't like the way we ended our last conversation," she said dropping her purse to the floor. Her hands were free, making Shannon nervous.

"Oh?" Shannon asked not so innocently.

"Yes, oh. Actually." She lazily surveyed Shannon's body like she had in Moab. "I was thinking maybe we could share a few Os ourselves."

Shannon had to stop herself from laughing. How corny—share a few Os ourselves? Good God, it was an outright proposition and she hadn't been hit on so blatantly since, well, since last night. Get real, Nikki. She wondered if Nikki thought about clichés all day or if she just made them up as she went along.

"Nikki, we already talked about this. I don't mix business with pleasure."

"No, sugar, you talked."

"And that's all we're going to do. I told you—"

"Yeah, yeah, I know. You don't do married women and you don't eat the hand that feeds you. No matter how good they would be."

Shannon smiled one of her quirky smiles, the one that typically diffused most situations. "Now, Nikki—" she started to say before she was interrupted by the door swinging open.

"There you are, baby. I thought I saw you come in here."

Shannon was never so glad to see Frank filling the doorway as she was right at this moment. "Frank, hey, Nikki was looking for you," she said nervously, not glancing at Nikki, knowing what she'd see reflected in her eyes.

"Bullshit," was his reply. "The only reason she's here is because you are."

Shannon's heart beat a little faster and her palms began to sweat. She doubted Frank Striker could kick her ass, but he sure could give her a big wedgie.

"She's a big fan of yours. Talks about you all the time. If I were the jealous type…" Frank was smiling broadly now.

Nikki stepped forward. "Thanks for the lesson, Shannon. And thank that other rider…what was her name again? Oh yeah, Caroline, for the excitement of the afternoon. She looked pretty good too."

Shannon didn't miss the innuendo in Nikki's statement and a wave of jealousy ran through her. If she made a move on Caroline…

"Get some sleep, Shannon. You've gotta win tomorrow," Frank said as he and Nikki walked out the door arm in arm but not before Nikki blew her a kiss over her shoulder.

Shannon sat in one of the chairs at the long table in the middle of the room. Nikki was not the first married woman to come on to her, and she wasn't the first wife of a sponsor to do so either. There was that time in France a few years ago when the wife of the event sponsor cornered her in the hotel bathroom. She had met her the night before at the sponsor event and the interest was unmistakable. She had chatted Shannon up all night, and toward the end of the evening when she followed Shannon into a stall in the ladies room and locked the door behind her, Shannon wasn't surprised. It really couldn't be called a stall at all. The walls went from the floor to the ceiling and the door was full length with slats that allowed you to look out but no one could see in.

There was plenty of room and the woman dropped immediately to her knees after a searing kiss that left Shannon's legs quivering and her clit throbbing. She knew she shouldn't be doing this, but as the woman worked her skillful tongue on her she couldn't think of one reason why not. Several women came and went, none of whom had any idea what was going on in the stall second from the end.

Shannon was normally a vocal lover, and the combination of the circumstances, the thrill of the place, and what was being done to her sent her over the edge. She came biting her tongue, her moan camouflaged by the sound of the hand dryer. When the woman washing her hands left, the woman between her legs stood and unlocked the door. She walked out of the stall, washed her hands and face, straightened her blouse, and calmly strolled out as if she hadn't just had her mouth on the most intimate place of a virtual stranger. Shannon had never had such an erotic experience before or since.

Shannon pulled her jacket over her shirt, the TKS logo embroidered on the back and over her left breast. She found it ironic that the clothing line Frank Striker made protected her from the scrapes and scratches on the trail, and she wondered if he made anything to protect her from his wife.

On her way back to the hotel she passed the expo village and the party was in full swing. The Saturday night before the final was always a night of adventure and excitement for everyone. Everyone except the most serious riders, that is. They needed to be sharp the next day or run the risk of smacking into a rock, catapulting over their handlebars, or worse yet, falling down a mountain. When she was first on tour she hadn't missed a Saturday night. If she somehow had not made the finals, she partied without hesitation. If she was on tap the following day, she still partied, but not with the abandon she normally would have. It was hell to fly down a rough, rock-strewn mountain with a headache. She kept walking, the sounds of laughter and music fading behind her.

CHAPTER TWELVE

Caroline was at the bottom of the lift waiting for her and her bike to be taken to the top of the mountain. The final day of the second race in the series was bright and clear and the crowds were enormous. The gondola operator recognized her and allowed her to sit alone on the wide bench instead of having to share with others. The chair could hold as many as four, but since she was alone, she sat dead center.

The nineteen-minute ride to the top was noisy. The hum of the cable pulling her and her fellow finalists, their bikes, and the hundreds of fans that dotted the course up and down the hill was steady. She could see most of the trail below her and watched as a rider made her way down the mountain, zigzagging around the hairpin turns, jumping over rocks, and vaulting over ditches. No one rode that good. No one could do what that woman was doing except one person, and Caroline watched intently as Shannon negotiated every turn and challenge. When she crossed the finish line, the roar of the crowd hurt her ears, even as far away as she was.

Caroline shuddered. It wasn't because it was cool at the top of the eight-thousand-foot mountain or because of the 360 degree view of the valley. She shuddered after watching Shannon conquer the mountain with the skill and grace rarely displayed by any other rider, male or female. Her bike was an extension of her body. Her legs connected to the pedals as if they were her own feet, the handlebars a lengthening of her arms, the machine flowing under her like a ballerina floating through the air.

It had been ten years and Shannon had only gotten more attractive with age. Where once was a lanky teenager, now was a stunningly gorgeous woman. Her shyness had been augmented with confidence almost verging on cockiness. Her hot looks were replaced with charisma and sex appeal. Either way, Shannon still had the ability to take her breath away, and she hated herself for it. She knew Shannon's reputation on the circuit. Hell, she had seen it in person. She had more women after her than anyone she had ever seen. Caroline was no prude, but even she drew the line at someone new in her bed in every city.

Maybe she was jealous. The thought of Shannon doing to another woman what she had done to her made it seem somehow cheap and superficial. Touch here, get moan in return. Run tongue down there and get quiver of response. Insert finger into slot A then remove. Repeat action until orgasm is achieved.

"What in the hell am I doing?" Caroline shouted into the thin air. Her seat bounced in reaction to her body's forceful question. "This is one of the biggest races of my life and I'm thinking about everything other than the next forty minutes of my life. I could get myself killed. Snap out of it, Caroline. Pull your head out of Shannon's crotch and concentrate." The last word finished just before she arrived at the summit.

Caroline smoothly stepped off the lift and gathered her thoughts back to where they should be—on the race ahead of her as she waited for her bike to be passed to her. She had to be on the top of her game or not only could she lose this event, she could hurt herself severely if she weren't careful. A broken collarbone, or any other major injury, and her chance at the championship was over.

Approaching the start line, Caroline closed her eyes and envisioned the course below. She had memorized the trail as described on the map and after the ten practice laps she had run over the past few days, she was comfortable with what she needed to do when. The course was challenging, to say the least; this was, after all, the world championship. Not a race for novices or the tentative. She would attack the mountain like she attacked everything and in the end would not say she didn't give it her best.

The bell sounded and in almost the blink of an eye she was approaching the bottom half of the course. The turns were tighter, the climbs steeper, the terrain rougher than at the top, and even more dangerous as the riders tired. Her front tire hit a mogul harder than she anticipated, the jolt absorbed by her front fork shock absorbers. Her right hand slipped off her grip and her handlebar veered to the left. Her front wheel threatened to spin out from under her and she struggled to maintain control. If she fell on this part of the course it would be more than a little painful, it would be disaster.

Crossing the finish line, Caroline knew she had not beaten Shannon's time. She turned and saw that her slip in that last turn had, in fact, cost her the race. She finished second to Shannon by seven tenths of a second. The crowd was cheering and she knew some of it was for her but most was for Shannon who was in the hot seat, the place just under the scoreboard where the leader sat until dethroned by the next fastest rider. She was half sitting, half standing against her bike, her helmet in one hand, a Gatorade in the other. The smile on her face said it all.

Before Caroline could turn away, Shannon looked directly at her. She was too far away to read the expression in her eyes, but her wide smile dropped ever so slightly before she nodded at Caroline. It was as if she were telling her something but Caroline had no idea what it was and quite frankly didn't care.

A crowd gathered around her and Caroline dismounted before she was knocked over. Congratulatory slaps on her back and "good race," "nice try," and "you'll get her in France" echoed from all directions. Twenty minutes later, one of the race sponsors somehow found her and took her bike and led her to the podium. Being the second place finisher, she would stand on the pedestal to the right of where Shannon would stand. The third place finisher would flank Shannon's other side.

Caroline drank from her water bottle while the pomp, circumstance, and speeches droned on. She was sweaty, hot, tired, and more than a little disappointed. She could have won this race if she had only had her complete attention on the race the entire time leading up to her final run. But no, she had to have a wet dream about Shannon and what it was like when she—a jolt in her side and a whistle brought her out of her daydreaming. Her name must have been called because everyone was looking at her, including the woman in third place. Tentatively, she stepped forward and onto the box with a big number two emblazoned on the front. She was handed a bouquet of flowers, and a medal was placed around her neck.

Caroline acknowledged Fran, who had managed to get no closer than three deep in the crowd. She was waving and whistling and jumping up and down. Fran didn't care she had come in second. Fran's enthusiasm was contagious and Caroline couldn't help but smile in return. It was only one race, after all. There were ten more to go, including the marathon twenty-four-hour race in Australia. She and Shannon were tied in points and she was only five tenths of a second behind her.

Caroline was acutely aware of Shannon standing next to her. Shannon's body was fit and firm and she filled out her bike shorts better than anyone Caroline had ever seen. Some riders chose to wear baggies, modified hiking shorts with the traditional bike short sewn in. Caroline had several pair herself but chose to wear the more fitted shorts in terrain like today's where branches could snag on the material and slow her down, or worse.

A tall, too thin blonde placed the medal around Shannon's neck and instead of kissing her on the cheek, she planted her lips directly on Shannon's. The crowd loved it, Shannon appeared to be surprised, and Caroline steamed.

"Ladies and gentlemen," the announcer's voice boomed over the public address system. "The winner of stage two of the world championship mountain bike series. Shannon Roberts."

Flashbulbs blinded Caroline and she smiled and waved to the crowd. It was expected of her and she played the part. What she really wanted to do was slap that grin off the blonde's face and push her down the mountain behind them. But she didn't, and after the interviews and pictures were finished, she and Fran walked to her sponsor's trailer.

"I can't believe she beat you. I was watching you on the JumboTron and I thought you had her."

Caroline pulled off her chest protector. Sweat, grime, and dirt had accumulated on her no-longer-white T-shirt and she washed her face in the sink. The trailer wasn't fancy, but simply a cargo trailer Striker used to store their gear at the races. It would be packed up by morning and on its way to Madrid.

"My hand slipped," Caroline said by way of explanation. "And my concentration," she murmured not quite soft enough.

"I heard that last part. What are you talking about? What got you off your mark?" Fran had been to enough races to know Caroline's pre-race routine and how sacred it was to her.

"Nothing." Caroline tried to change the subject.

"Don't give me that. Your concentration is as legendary as your technical skill. What's going on? You never make a careless mistake like that."

"Jeez, Fran, you make it sound like I'm a machine and mistakes never happen. My hand slipped; that's all."

"Other people make mistakes, not Caroline Davis," Fran said standing with her arms folded across her chest.

"Yeah, well, Caroline Davis isn't perfect, no matter how much you'd like her to be. I lost, but next week is Madrid and after that France and Andorra. I'll beat her in every race through Europe so that by the time we get to Switzerland, I'll be so far in front of her she'll need a compass to even get close to me."

"She's gotten under your skin."

"No, she hasn't," Caroline snapped. "Get over it, Fran. I have. Let me repeat myself for the last time. There is nothing going on between me and Shannon Roberts. What was is long over and nothing but a high school crush. I have moved on, and by her reputation, she has too." Caroline slammed the lid of the equipment box. "Now shut up about it."

CHAPTER THIRTEEN

Caroline was true to her word and she finished ahead of Shannon in France, Madrid, and Italy. Shannon had beaten her in Germany, Andorra, and South Africa. At the end of eight races, Caroline had fifty-five points to Shannon's fifty-three. Having the highest number of points, Caroline was wearing the blue jersey for this race. Nine weeks had passed since she tore Fran's head off during their argument in Scotland, and she was due to arrive at the end of the week.

The flight from South Africa to Geneva was a marathon twenty-one hours of travel time and three different flights. She was battling jet lag, fatigue, and unsuccessfully trying to avoid Shannon. Shannon seemed to be everywhere she went. It didn't matter if Caroline was in Madrid, Munich, or Florence, Shannon was in the restaurant, at the required sponsor event, on the practice track. This was their week off with no races and she needed time to rest, practice, and be alone. The Swiss resort in downtown Champéry was the perfect place.

Located ninety minutes from Geneva, Champéry was the picture postcard of a small village in the Swiss Alps. The Les Dents du Midi Mountains framed the village and its chalets and hotels. The town consisted of narrow streets lined with small shops and restaurants catering to the international clientele that came to Champéry in the winter for its excellent skiing and the summer for beautiful outdoor activities.

The ninth race was being held at the Bike Park, the largest mountain bike domain in Europe. Formed by the Swiss resorts of the Portes du

Soleil, Champéry, Val d'Illiez, and Morgins, the park boasted twenty-four lifts, nine downhill trails, and hundreds of miles of marked trails. If the opportunity to ride the fabulous trails didn't make your heart stop, the stunning views of the Swiss Alps would.

Caroline skidded to a stop after her second practice run down Trail 105, the official downhill track this year. As she had expected and didn't want, Shannon was waiting for her at the bottom of the course.

"Good ride."

"Thanks." Caroline unbuckled her helmet and pulled off her gloves. Sweat dripped down the side of her forehead and trickled down her cheek. She wiped at it with a shaking hand. Caroline didn't see Shannon's bike in the vicinity and wondered what Shannon wanted. She let her do the talking.

"When did you get here?"

"Yesterday."

"Are you staying at the Hotel Suisse?" Shannon shifted her weight from foot to foot.

"No. I'm at the Chalet Eden. My parents and a friend of mine are coming in." Shannon wondered if the "friend" was the woman she saw Caroline with in Canada and Germany. She didn't like it but held her opinion to herself. She didn't know why she was here, but when she saw Caroline's name on the practice sheet she found herself at the bottom of the mountain waiting for her.

"How are the folks?" Shannon asked with more than a bit of irony. She could see Caroline's father's face when he was standing in that doorway like it was ten minutes ago.

"Fine," Caroline answered hesitantly.

"Do you have time to get some lunch?" Shannon blurted out before she realized it. The expression on Caroline's face said she was equally surprised.

"Just lunch. I'm not going to try to pump you on information about your gear or your strategy." Shannon tried to laugh but it came out more of a choke than anything else. She had no idea why she'd asked Caroline to lunch or even why she wanted to spend any time with her. They had been at the same races for several years and had kept their distance, so what was it about now that changed? Maybe it was seeing her with her father again that brought back all the memories.

"Shannon, I don't know."

"It's just lunch. It's not as if we're strangers." That was an understatement.

"But we're adversaries." Caroline's tone was cautious.

"So? Do you think I'm going to feed you bad food so you'll be barfing instead of beating me?" This time when she laughed it came out as expected. "Come on, Caroline. We haven't spoken to each other in ten years. We're grown women now. Let's catch up." God, it even sounded lame to her own ears.

Shannon watched Caroline struggle with her invitation. Maybe she would say sure, what the hell, let's catch up. Maybe she'd say no because her girlfriend wasn't here. Maybe she'd say yes for the same reason.

"All right," Caroline answered hesitantly.

Shannon jumped on it before she had a chance to change her mind. "How about I meet you at the Verita Café, say, eleven thirty?" That was an hour from now, giving Caroline enough time for another ride if she wanted and a quick shower. Shannon thought she looked fine just as she was, dirt and all.

"Eleven thirty," Caroline said and pedaled off toward the chair lift. Shannon watched her secure her bike and sit in the chair. Just as the lift began, Caroline turned and looked directly at Shannon, her face betraying nothing.

The back of Caroline's head floated farther and farther away as the gondola took her to the top of the mountain. Except this time, Shannon knew she'd be back.

❖

She looked at her watch at least a dozen times before Caroline finally walked through the door. The closer it got to the time they had agreed to meet, the more Shannon began to doubt that Caroline would actually show up. She wasn't used to this uncertainty. The women she went out with always showed up. As a matter of fact, most times they were early and Shannon was the one they waited for. It felt odd to have the shoe on the other foot. She didn't like it.

For the past year, thoughts of Caroline had crossed her mind more and more often. She wondered just how different her life would have been if they had stayed together. Would it be any different? Would she still have bounced around from woman to woman never staying long enough to learn more than just her name?

She was the bad girl on the circuit. It was her persona even though just as much was conjecture as reality. She was tired. Tired of the travel, the junk food, and the endless empty nights. Who knew she was seriously thinking about retiring and settling down? But what surprised her the most was how often thoughts of Caroline popped in her head.

The chiming of the bell above the door rang again as another patron entered with Caroline right behind him. Shannon barely glanced at the man, her complete focus on Caroline. She had changed into a tangerine-colored sleeveless blouse over matching plaid shorts that fell just above her knees, accentuating her long legs. A tattoo that hadn't been there ten years ago circled one pale ankle above camel and tan boat shoes. Shannon wondered if Caroline had any more surprises hidden under her fashionable clothes.

When Caroline saw her, Shannon's heart jumped a beat or two faster at the flash of recognition in her eyes. That expression didn't last long as Caroline quickly covered it up. But Shannon knew it was there. It reminded her of every time they saw each other those many years ago.

Caroline took a deep breath as she approached the table where her ex-lover sat. Funny, she thought, she had never really thought of or referred to Shannon as an ex-lover. It sounded so intimate. But wasn't that what they had been? Intimate? No, she shook her head. Sex, fucking, and lust are what you have when you're seventeen. The word "lover" just sounds too mature for teenagers.

All of this and much more raced through her head as she closed the gap between them. Shannon stood as she approached and Caroline's reaction to her was as thrilling today as it was all those other times that seemed like ages ago.

Caroline was a freshman when she first saw Shannon walk across the courtyard of MHA. At first she thought she was an upperclassman, the way she walked with confidence, as if she had always belonged at the prestigious school. Her hair was longer than it was today and equally blond and unruly. She had the swagger of someone who went after what she wanted and the sophistication that only the wealthy seem to inherit. Caroline had started to suspect she was attracted to girls and one look at Shannon Roberts confirmed it. But it wasn't until two years later and that fateful summer that changed her life.

Caroline was a virgin when she and Shannon finally got together. She knew all about the boy/girl thing but had no idea what to put where to make a girl cry out and beg for more. But with Shannon she caught on fast. It was as if she had been pulled out of a fog that she only thought she was seeing through. With Shannon, every day was brighter, every minute an adventure. As in typical teenage fashion, Shannon was everything to her and Caroline thought she couldn't live without her. But obviously she had. They both had, and here they were all these months and years later. And Caroline felt as she did back then.

"You seem surprised to see me," Caroline said. Shannon pulled out the chair for her.

The waiter arrived and took their drink order, giving Shannon a reprieve from answering. But Caroline wasn't letting her off the hook. "Didn't think I'd show up?" *And why is she so relieved that I did?*

"I wasn't sure if you would or not," Shannon admitted.

"I said I'd come." Caroline tried to relax. The conversation felt forced and awkward and it got worse with a long pause when neither she nor Shannon said anything. Shannon looked anything but the sophisticated, cocky poster girl of the circuit. She looked scared to death. Caroline took pity on her.

"How have you been, Shannon?" *What have you been doing with yourself? How do you spend your days? Who do you spend your nights with? Do you ever think of me? Did you fall apart like I did when you left?* Those and a dozen other questions threatened to spill out of her mouth. Her pride kept them in.

"No complaints, I suppose. How about you? I was sorry to hear about your crash." Shannon toyed with her spoon, a sign of nervousness Caroline remembered.

"I'm okay now. It was a nasty spill and I still have two pins in my leg, but it only bothers me when it's really cold, or when I sit too long." Actually, it bothered her more than she cared to admit, but a steady dose of ibuprofen and ice kept the major discomfort at bay.

The waiter returned with their drinks and Caroline ordered a roast beef sandwich with chips and Shannon ordered a rare burger and fries. There was another long pause when he left.

"Why did you invite me to lunch?" By the look on Shannon's face, Caroline might as well have asked her to recite the entire periodic table of elements. "We haven't spoken to each other since high school. Why now? Why this race?" Why did you leave me? Why didn't you stay and fight for me? Why didn't you ever call me?

"I don't know. I guess I thought it was time." Shannon squirmed in her seat.

"Time for what?" Caroline was surprised when long dormant anger simmered to the surface. She had been angry at the way Shannon had left her. Angry that she never made more of an effort to contact her. Angry that she had practically ignored her at every race they competed in. It wasn't as if she had fallen off the face of the earth.

"Jesus, Caroline, would you give me a break here? I know it's been a long time, but that was years ago."

"And we're supposed to act like, what…we let bygones be bygones? It never happened?" Caroline could just as well forget what it was like to make love with Shannon as she could her own shoe size. That was the trouble. She couldn't forget. At the rate she was going she'd never forget.

"No, of course not," Shannon replied quickly, finally showing some spark in the conversation.

"Of course not what? We let it go? Or act like it never happened?" Their food came and the waiter left without saying a word, the tension between the two of them obvious.

"Neither one." It was Shannon's turn to be angry. "For Christ sake, Caroline, why don't you flay me open right here, right now? Will that make you feel better? It was years ago. An entire lifetime ago and I'm sorry." She raised her hand cutting off what Caroline was about to say. "I'm sorry that was the way your father found out. I'm sorry that you were put in that position. I'm sorry that you had to deal with all of it. But what I'm not sorry about is that we were together in the first place." Shannon took a long drink of her tea.

"Is it too much to want to talk, to find out how you are, what you've been doing with your life? I don't want to pretend like it never happened, Caroline, because it did. We had a teenage fling. It was

intense, it was powerful, and it was a defining moment in our lives."
Shannon hesitated. "At least it was for me. You can't simply pretend it
didn't happen. Well, maybe you can, but I can't."

Shannon took a breath expecting Caroline to interrupt and was
surprised when she didn't. She just sat there looking at her as if she
were crazy. "What?"

"What do you want from me, Shannon?" Caroline was tired of
dancing around the two of them. It was *the* main question she had been
asking herself for weeks, especially knowing she'd see her every day
for weeks instead of once or twice a year. The tension in her shoulders
and the butterflies in the pit of her stomach were all the evidence she
needed that Shannon still had the ability to affect her.

"I just want to talk with you. Tell me what you've been doing with
yourself, how you are."

"Talk to you. You want me to talk to you." Shannon nodded. "Fine.
After I left MHA I went to Columbia. My undergrad and graduate
degrees are in physics and I defend my dissertation for my Ph.D. in
astrophysics three weeks after the tour ends. I've been accepted to the
astronaut program at NASA. I train in Colorado and have a cracker-box
apartment in New York. I have good friends, my baby sister has five
kids, God help her, and my parents love me. Other than what you know
about me and the tour, that about sums it up." Caroline sat back in the
booth. There were a few more words about her life after that fateful day
her father opened her dorm room door, but she was not going to share
them with Shannon. She hadn't told anyone except for Fran, and that
was just recently.

"NASA? You're going to be an astronaut?"

Out of everything she said, this was Shannon's follow-up question?
Nothing about how I was after she left me? What did my father say?
Did he hit me or scream at me? Did I curl up in a ball and cry? Did I
miss her? Shannon had the reputation of being a party girl on the tour,
not serious about anything, no commitments other than the next race,
and she sure was showing her colors now. "Yes, I am." Caroline had
always dreamed of walking in space or being the first woman to step
foot on the moon.

"That's cool. And Ashley has five kids?"

"Yes, one right after the other."

Shannon asked a few more basic questions that Caroline answered in simple sentences or with a yes or no. She didn't feel particularly chatty and certainly didn't trust either Shannon's motives or her own body's response. She kept herself on a tight leash during the stilted conversation.

"I got an invitation to our ten-year reunion," Shannon said referring to their time together at MHA for the first time.

"I did too."

"Are you going?" Shannon asked, hiding behind a French fry going into her mouth.

If I say yes, will you ask me to go as your date, Caroline wanted to say, but instead answered truthfully. "No. I'll be at NASA then and I'm not interested in going."

"Why not? It might be fun going back and seeing what everyone has turned into. Who has the most kids, the biggest house in the Hamptons, the ugliest husband." She chuckled.

"I haven't kept in touch with anyone from MHA, so I don't really care what they're up to." The two weeks between being discovered and graduation were the longest of her young life. Somehow word must have gotten out that she and Shannon were caught together because she was ostracized by girls that had been her friends the day before and others had given her a silent thumbs up in the cafeteria. Either way, the only thing good that came out of MHA was that it got her accepted to Columbia.

Shannon didn't know what to say next. She had tried casual conversation, current events, the tour, and had even brought up MHA, but nothing made Caroline talk with her like she had years ago.

"I thought maybe we could go as friends."

"You're kidding, right?" An image flashed in her mind of heads turning when she walked in with Shannon Roberts on her arm.

When she didn't respond, Caroline continued.

"You want us to be friends? Like have lunch once in a while and chat about the weather or whether a carbon or aluminum frame is stronger or how much travel we have in our front shocks? Are you out of your mind?"

Anger and embarrassment filled Shannon's stomach and she wanted to throw up. This had gone terribly wrong. What was supposed to be a nice get reacquainted lunch had turned sour very fast. If it didn't start out that way to begin with. Caroline was right about one thing—what in the hell had she been thinking? She let anger take control.

"I guess I must be to think that you were mature enough to handle this. But obviously I was wrong. I'm sorry if I've ruined your lunch and upset you. You won't have to worry about me bothering you again." Shannon tossed money on the table and walked away.

CHAPTER FOURTEEN

On Friday of race weekend the expo was in full operation. Every manufacturer of bicycle gear, frames, components, sports drinks, energy bars, and nature trails was represented. The tents were set up surrounding the winner's circle and people were milling about, some carrying packages bearing the logo of their purchase. Fifteen feet from the Gatorade tent was autograph central, where riders were assigned shifts and signed autographs for fans passing T-shirts, hats, and pictures across the table to their favorite rider.

Shannon was stationed at the table with one of the male riders and she was attracting much more business than he was. The people that came to these events were typically in their late teens and twenties with an occasional thirtysomething attending as well. Shannon signed autographs, recognizing a few familiar faces of those fans that had been at previous events. These people must have money to be able to follow the circuit, she thought as she scrawled her name across her image embossed on a white tank top. One after another, they stood in line patiently waiting their turn to offer a compliment, share a word or two with her, or ask a question.

"I think you're the best rider on the tour," the fan gushed. She wasn't much older than twenty and by the look of adoration on her face Shannon could be between her legs within the hour if she were so inclined. But she wasn't interested, which was a surprise. Shannon had usually scored at least once, sometimes twice, at races, but for the first time in a long time she had no desire to fuck a total stranger no matter how attractive she was.

"Thanks, enjoy the event," Shannon said coolly but politely. The young thing sported a pout of disappointment and moved on.

"I think you squashed her plans for the night, or at a minimum hurt her feelings."

Shannon cringed inside and glanced at her watch before looking up to see Nikki standing in front of her. Perfect timing, she thought, her one-hour shift was over.

"I don't know what you're talking about." Shannon stood; her back was sore from sitting on the hard metal chair.

Nikki moved to the end of the table effectively blocking her exit. "Sure you do, sugar. She wanted a piece of you, the infamous Shannon Roberts, mountain bike rider extraordinaire, famous lover on the tour."

Shannon detected a whiff of something alcoholic on Nikki's breath and her stomach turned. She was hard enough to handle lately, but the addition of alcohol was a new and potentially dangerous development.

"She's just a kid," Shannon said, unsuccessfully maneuvering around Nikki without touching her.

Nikki turned at the exact moment Shannon passed, her arms skimmed the tip of Nikki's man-made breasts. She heard her sharp intake of breath before Nikki said, "Oh, yes, I liked that. I definitely like that."

"Have you seen Frank? I have to talk to him." Shannon tried to deflect the conversation. She knew it was pointless, but she tried nonetheless.

"He's in a meeting with somebody," Nikki replied. She stepped in front of Shannon. "He won't be finished for at least another hour."

Her insinuation was clear and Shannon was tired of Nikki chasing her like a bitch in heat. She was not interested and the more she pushed, the more disgusted Shannon became. She wanted to slap her, or at the very least scream at her to leave her alone. She bit back what she really wanted to say.

"Okay, thanks. That'll give me enough time to talk to Norm. My gears are slipping between five and six and he'll know what to do," Shannon lied through her teeth. There was nothing wrong with her bike. Even if there was, she could fix it better than the THS mechanic Frank kept on staff. "If you'll excuse me." Shannon quickly sidestepped her. She didn't relax until she had turned the corner and was heading back toward her hotel. Even then she kept glancing over her shoulder, expecting to see Nikki following her.

The sliding doors opened silently and a whish of cool air blew over her skin. It was hot and more than a little humid and she had practically run the half mile from the expo to her hotel. She veered to the left and within five minutes had a lukewarm beer in one hand, a glass of ice in the other, and a bowl of pretzels between them.

The hotel lounge was crowded, another sign that one of the biggest events in Switzerland was in town. She had managed to get to a table in the back of the room without being recognized and she sat with her back to the wall watching the scene in front of her. Even though it was considered a big no-no by beer aficionados, Shannon preferred her beer ice cold and expertly poured the beverage over the ice and waited for the small head of foam to subside. Studying the room, she recognized more than a few fellow riders, both male and female, all sporting their sponsor logos like the money on their back it was.

Not long after she sat down, a pair who had been all over each other in one of the dark booths in the corner practically ran out of the lounge to what Shannon guessed was one of their rooms. Hooking up was one of the pastimes of riders at every race. Some did it to kill time, others to alleviate the stress of the ride, and others simply because they could. One rider went so far as to call his liaisons his "weekend wife." Shannon wondered if his "weekday wife" was savvy to his escapades. She doubted it. What happens on the circuit stays on the circuit. At least as far as the riders were concerned. It was the worst kept secret as to who was fucking whom, but nobody said anything about it outside of the tour.

She was into her third beer when Caroline walked in with the woman Shannon had seen her with in Scotland. Fran had also been with Caroline in Madrid, France, and Germany and Shannon couldn't help noticing how close they were. She had watched them together, Fran handing Caroline her gear, wiping off her goggles, and even straightening her shirt. The act was almost intimate, implying that they were more than just friends.

A surge of jealousy crept into her throat and she unsuccessfully tried to wash it down with her beer. She signaled the waitress for another and couldn't stop herself from watching the two of them squeeze through the patrons at the bar. Fran was leading, holding on to Caroline's hand with what looked like a firm grip pulling her deeper into the crowd. Finally they had their drinks and Caroline looked relieved to get out of the crowd and into a booth.

As they laughed and talked, Shannon saw Fran touch Caroline's hand more than a few times to emphasize a point or God knows what. Every time she touched Caroline or laughed at something Caroline said, the hair on the back of Shannon's neck stood up. She had no right to feel this way about Caroline. She was free to socialize with whomever she wanted, but Shannon hated it nonetheless.

She was jealous, pure and simple. For no good reason other than she was. She couldn't pinpoint why and didn't even try. She had never been jealous of anyone before and it was an uncomfortable sensation. She wanted to rip Fran's head off, and if she touched Caroline one more time she might have to cut her hand off at the wrist.

Without warning, Caroline looked her way and caught Shannon staring at them. *Shit.* The last thing she needed was for Caroline to know how she felt, but by the look on her face, she did. Faking bravado she didn't feel, Shannon raised her glass as if to say "here's to you and your girlfriend." She drained the half glass of beer without stopping to take a breath. The waitress must have been watching her as she appeared out of nowhere and Shannon nodded for her to bring another.

Against her better judgment, Shannon drank the beer knowing she would feel groggy and sluggish in the morning. She didn't have to race until after two, but she had enough experience chasing away hangovers to know exactly what to do to be in shape for her race. An espresso, two tall glasses of pure orange juice with extra pulp, a poached egg, three slices of bacon, and she'd be ready to go.

Several times Shannon caught Caroline looking her way and then quickly turning her attention back to Fran. Was she the type of girl to cheat? Shannon didn't think so, but what in the hell did she know about her? She never would have thought she'd be sitting here in Geneva, Switzerland, a favorite to win the world championship, but here she was. Things definitely change in ten years. But then again—she studied the shape of Caroline's legs, the curve of her breast, the way her face lit up when she smiled—some things never change.

❖

The bright lights of the bathroom were not pretty on Shannon's bruised and battered skin. Road rash covered her left arm from the top of her shoulder to her wrist. Blood had seeped through the bandage around her elbow and would need to be changed soon. The crash during her second run had ended Shannon's day in a very painful way.

Her riding gloves had protected her hands, but her fingers hurt as she opened and closed her fist. Moving down to her legs, the knee pad and shin guard had taken most of the damage, but a purple bruise was already forming on the outside of her left knee. A matching bruise was well under way on her hip spreading to the middle of her ass cheek. Somehow, she had a scrape on her right cheek, a fat lip, and she would have a doozy of a shiner on her right eye by morning. All in all, it could have been much worse. She could have broken her neck or her collarbone at a minimum. The result of going ass-end-over-tin-cups, as her grandfather used to say, was not pretty.

Shannon's entire body ached when she reached to turn on the water in the tub. She would have preferred a shower, but the aide at the health center had washed off most of the dirt and grime and she doubted if she could stand the force of the water against her raw skin. Shannon downed three ibuprofen with a beer from the minibar, unconcerned with the potential side effects of mixing alcohol and medication. Hopefully, it would knock her unconscious for the night because sleeping was probably out of the question.

She ignored the knock at the door and watched the hot water slowly fill the large Jacuzzi tub. Any other time she would slide in and let the jets work their magic, but just the thought of them bombarding her flesh sent a chill down her spine.

Cursing the persistent knocking, she limped to the door. "Go away. I don't want anything, and I'm in no mood for company." She peered through the peephole and into the concerned eyes of Caroline.

"I'm not going away, so you might as well let me in," came the muffled reply.

Shannon couldn't see Caroline's body language, but her tone definitely said she was not taking no for an answer. Sighing, she slid open the safety chain and turned the knob.

Caroline held back a sob at the sight of Shannon's face peeking out from behind the door. She was pale, her face clearly showing the pain she must be in. "I came to check on you."

"You did, I'm alive, now go away and leave me alone."

She started to shut the door but Caroline refused to be dismissed. Shannon had taken a nasty spill on the last run and, along with the crowd, Caroline had held her breath until Shannon gave them a thumbs up while being carried to the first aid tent.

"Not a chance. Let me in or I'll knock you over, and you know I can." She watched as Shannon debated with herself as to whether or not to obey. When she stepped aside Caroline knew she had won—this round.

What she wasn't prepared for was that Shannon was totally naked and not even trying to cover herself. Her lustful thoughts were quickly replaced by concern and horror at the sight of her injuries.

"My God, Shannon. How are you even able to walk? Let me help you." Caroline dropped her bag on the floor, hurried over, and froze when she didn't know how to help or where to touch her where it wouldn't hurt.

"I was just getting into the tub," Shannon said, indicating the open door to what Caroline guessed was the bathroom.

"Good idea." She stood with her hands up trying to find a place on Shannon's body that wasn't bruised or scraped. She settled on taking her hand and wrapping her arm around her waist. Slowly, they walked the short distance to the tub.

The water was about three-quarters full and Caroline turned off the spigots. The last of the water dripped into the tub with a drip, drip, drip. "Can you get in?"

Shannon lifted her injured leg and banged her ankle on the side of the tall tub. "Ouch, shit. The goddamned tub is too high. I can't even lift my leg over the edge."

Still holding Shannon, Caroline surveyed the situation. The tub was on a pedestal of sorts. It was designed more for sensuality than functionality and she knew there was no way Shannon would be able to get in or out on her own. There was only one thing to do.

"Okay, hang on." She kicked off her shoes, pulled her shirt over her head, and started pulling down her shorts.

"What are you doing?" Shannon watched her in the mirror on the wall adjacent to the tub.

"Getting in with you," Caroline answered as if it were the most obvious thing in the world. "You can't do it yourself and I don't feel like falling in when I'm helping you." She was now as naked as Shannon. "Is there a problem?"

Caroline watched as Shannon's eyes roamed over her body. They had seen each other naked hundreds of times but never as grown women. Time and hard work had transformed her body from girlish to all woman, and by the look on Shannon's face, she had done a fine job of it. She knew the look of desire in Shannon's eyes and her body heated under the intense approval.

"Stop it, Shannon. You can barely stand on your own two feet and you're getting into this tub right now." Caroline stepped into the warm water first then helped Shannon in. Caroline lowered herself and Shannon into the frothy water, her back sliding down the porcelain side.

Shannon moaned as her raw skin came in contact with the warm water. Caroline knew the sound wasn't from ecstasy but agony and she ached for the pain Shannon must be in. "I know it hurts," she said stupidly. This time Shannon hissed and cursed.

"Just try to relax." That was the second stupid thing she said.

"Easy for you to say," Shannon snapped.

Caroline didn't know what to do with her hands so she cupped them with water and poured it down Shannon's back.

"Thanks. I think that's the only place on my body that doesn't hurt. At least right now. Tomorrow, however, will be a totally different story."

Caroline repeated the motion several times and on the last handful followed the trail of water with the palms of her hands massaging the tight muscles in Shannon's back.

Her heart raced and her pulse beat loudly in her head each time she touched Shannon. Her skin was soft and slick from the water, her fingers gliding over the firm, tan flesh. The patch of skin that was much lighter than the rest of her back was just where she remembered it—just below her right shoulder blade. Caroline remembered when she first discovered the birthmark and how she had traced the shape with her fingertip first, then with her tongue. She shuddered at the memory and the water suddenly got much hotter.

"Caroline?" Shannon asked, piercing her haze of arousal. "I don't feel too good."

Shannon's comment and the weakness of her voice jolted Caroline out of her trip down memory lane. "Lean back against me for a minute." It was the only thing she could think of. She surely couldn't lift Shannon out of the tub if she passed out. Maybe if she sat back for a few minutes she would feel good enough to at least help Caroline get her out.

All medicinal thought flew out of her head when Shannon's back made contact with her breasts. Her nipples were already hard and had excellent recall of Shannon's body and tightened even harder. When Shannon's head dropped back on her shoulder, Caroline swallowed hard and forced herself to maintain her composure.

Shannon's hair was just under her nose, the scent not an unpleasant combination of strawberry and dirt. Her arms rested on the side of the tub and her nipples peeked out from the water with each rise and fall from her breathing. Caroline's legs were on either side of Shannon, her left one bent at the knee so as not to come in contact with Shannon's injured leg.

Any other time Caroline would be taking advantage of their position, and on more than one occasion in the past, she had. But this time Shannon was hurt, seriously hurt, but the way her body was reacting to Shannon's closeness—her familiarity, her nakedness pressed against her—it didn't seem to know that. Caroline had thought Shannon had fallen asleep and jerked when she spoke.

"I think I should get out. The drugs they gave me at the clinic are putting me to sleep and I'd hate to slide down and drown. However nice it would be to die in your arms."

Shannon was starting to slur her words and Caroline wasn't sure she heard the last part correctly. She wanted to ask but didn't dare. Instead, she pushed Shannon into a sitting position. "You're right. The water is getting cold and we've still got to change your bandages and get you into bed."

Caroline stood, her legs shaky from the inactivity as well as the sight in front of her. She grabbed a towel from the stack on the shelf above her head, quickly wiping off her hands and arms.

"Okay, let's get you up. On three. Ready?" As she counted, Caroline put her hands under Shannon's arms and lifted. She froze when Shannon screamed. "Oh my God, Shannon, what is it?"

Shannon's breathing was coming in short, fast pants. It took her several moments before she was able to answer. "It just hurts," she finally said.

"What? Where?" Caroline's heart was still in her throat, her own breathing shallow and quick.

"Everything. It's all right, just get me out of here."

Five minutes later Shannon was lying in the large bed, the covers drawn up over her nakedness. Caroline was wrapping the last of the gauze around her elbow, its whiteness a stark contrast to the red, raw skin.

"There, that should do it." She secured the last piece of tape. Caroline looked into dark eyes slightly glazed from pain and medication. "Try to get some sleep." She had an overwhelming urge to kiss Shannon's forehead like her mother used to when she was sick. She stopped herself as she started to lean toward her.

"Thanks." Shannon's voice was barely a whisper. As she fell asleep, Caroline gave in to the need and placed a light kiss just above her eyebrows.

Chapter Fifteen

Caroline watched the rhythmic rise and fall of Shannon's chest for the next several hours. It felt like her heart stopped every time she relived the scene of Shannon missing the turn and tumbling headfirst into the stand of trees. Due to the JumboTron at the finish line, all twelve thousand people in attendance saw it as well. The eerie quiet after the screech of horror was nerve-wracking until Shannon waved from the litter she was carried on. She was taken immediately to the on-site clinic. Caroline had no idea of her condition until after she received the third place medal and practically bolted off the stand in the direction of the first aid tent. She was stopped before she could enter, but the man on the door told her that Shannon was conscious and all of her limbs were moving. Caroline almost collapsed in relief.

She couldn't help but notice Shannon's body both when she was in the tub and as she helped her into bed. She was thin almost to the point of being skinny, every muscle defined and hard. She had a tattoo of an abstract female bike rider going downhill on the outside of her right calf and a series of symbols on her left. Her breasts were small and Caroline's palms tingled as if remembering just how perfectly they fit in them.

No matter how much she wanted to forget, various things over the past ten years reminded her of Shannon and at the oddest times. A flavor of ice cream, a movie title, even the words to a song flashed feelings of warmth or pain through her gut.

Caroline had no idea what she was doing here, in Shannon's room. Well, she did, but *why* was the question. Other racers she knew had been injured, some more severely than Shannon, and she never felt the unrelenting need to see how they were. She needed to verify with her own eyes that Shannon was all right. She hadn't even bothered to change out of her riding shorts and shirt. She had dropped her safety gear off at the trailer and found Fran to tell her where she was going. They were supposed to meet back at the Shimano tent after the awards ceremony and interviews and head back to the hotel together. But Fran nodded her understanding and Caroline found herself at Shannon's door soon thereafter.

As she watched her sleep, Caroline thought back on their conversation earlier in the week. What was Shannon trying to do? What was her intention? What did she want from her? She admitted she hadn't given her a chance to say much, but laid into her instead. She didn't realize that she was still angry and hurt over the way it ended between them. Good God, it was ten years ago and she was seventeen at the time. What did she expect? Some sort of nice, neat closure? It had been anything but. And why hadn't Shannon called? Caroline had asked herself that question hundreds of times over the following year, each time imagining what she would say to Shannon when she did.

She had called Shannon until the numbers wore off her phone. She used mutual friends to get in touch with her, but for two weeks all they were able to do was trade voicemails. It was frustrating and when they finally did connect their conversation was forced and stilted. They used to talk about everything, but during that last conversation they had almost nothing to talk about. It was amazing that at seventeen how quickly things went from great to over. Caroline buried her hurt in training and driving herself to exhaustion studying for her Ph.D.

And now here she was. Five feet from the woman who at one time meant everything to her—or at least she thought she did. But that was a lifetime ago when she thought Shannon was the love of her life. That they were going to spend the rest of their lives together. But when she had heard via the rumor mill that Shannon was with someone else, she knew it was simply a teenage thing. Here one day, gone another. So what was she doing here now, hovering over Shannon's every breath, worrying herself sick that she would be okay? While Shannon slept she had watched her, looked at her, and fought the urge to touch her.

The feelings that overwhelmed her all those years ago came back in tidal waves, one after the other. The joy, the happiness, waking every day knowing Shannon Roberts was in her life. It felt as if those years between never happened, that they were still together, finishing each other's sentences, knowing what the other wanted almost before she did, holding each other tight in passion. What in the hell was she supposed to do now?

❖

Shannon was falling, faster and faster down the hill until there was nothing under her but the thin air between her and the ground some eight feet below. She was suffocating and every muscle on her body screamed in agony as she struggled to sit up. "Shh, it's okay. You're okay, Shannon. You're safe." A familiar voice seeped past the thick fog of her subconscious. The darkness came again, ending her tormenting dreams.

When she woke again, this time more fully awake, Shannon didn't move, giving herself a chance to gather her wits. She hurt. God, did she hurt. Her left arm throbbed and it felt like her entire left side was lying on hot coals. Her head pounded. The light coming in from the window was the soft rays of dawn.

Cautiously, she turned her head, waiting for the pain to subside before focusing her attention on Caroline, who was in the chair beside the bed. She was curled on her right side as much as possible in the rocker recliner, her hair falling over one side of her face. She was wearing a terrycloth robe with the emblem of the hotel near her right breast. The front gaped open revealing her chest and the swell of her other breast. Her feet were bare, her toenails polished bright red.

Shannon smiled at the sight, the nail pedicure a complete contradiction to the mud and dirt of mountain bike racing. Then it all came back to her with agonizing clarity. She had somehow missed the last turn and remembered falling but nothing after that until the bright lights of the first aid tent. They had poked and prodded, x-rayed her from head to toe and, finding no injuries other than a severe case of road rash, had let her go. She had to fight like hell and sign a dozen forms releasing the clinic from responsibility if complications arose, but Shannon was determined not to spend the night in the local hospital.

She remembered getting back to her room and running a bath when Caroline arrived and wouldn't leave. Shannon's body flushed with heat as she remembered Caroline climbing into the tub with her, her hands gently stroking her back, the feel of the erect nipples when she lay against her. Shannon moved in reaction to the sensation and couldn't stop the moan of pain from escaping her parched lips. Caroline was instantly awake and alert.

"Shannon? Are you okay?"

The concern on Caroline's face was almost heartbreaking. She didn't want Caroline to hurt over her. Not again. Never again. "I'm fine, just a little sore. And thirsty. Can I have some water?"

"Sure." Caroline jumped out of the chair, her robe gaping open even more giving Shannon a glimpse of what she had seen last night. She wasn't that out of it not to remember how Caroline had looked standing naked in front of her. She had filled out into a beautiful woman, and no matter how banged up and battered she was, Shannon's body took notice.

"Here, let me help you sit up."

With Caroline's arm around her good shoulder Shannon was able to sit but not without a lot of pain, her head swimming more than once. Her hand shook when she reached for the glass and Caroline wrapped her own around Shannon's as she put the glass to her lips. The liquid was cool and felt wonderful filling her mouth and sliding down her dry throat. After several swallows, Caroline moved the glass away.

"Not too much. Let's see how this sits before you have any more."

"I'm just banged up, nothing life threatening." Shannon's voice was stronger this time.

"I don't care. You are banged up but that doesn't mean you can act like it's nothing. You might have a concussion."

"I don't have a concussion, just a headache where my head hit a damn tree or something." Caroline paled at her flippant remark and Shannon realized just how affected Caroline was by her spill. "Really, Caroline, I'm fine. Just a little tingle that a few aspirin will take care of." She was rewarded by Caroline's laugh.

"Yeah, and I'm the King of England. Come on, Shannon, how are you feeling? Besides the road rash of course."

Caroline was looking up and down her body as if checking to make sure she really was all right. "Honestly, I'm fine. A little stiff and my arm burns like hell, but nothing that a little time and a new layer of skin can't cure." As much as she wanted to lie in bed all day and look at Caroline, she had other pressing matters that were demanding her attention.

"I do have to go to the bathroom though." She tossed the covers off and swung her legs off the bed. Slowly, she stood, careful not to move too quickly or cause too much to hurt. "No, don't get up; I can do it," she said quickly as Caroline started to help her. Bandages covered pretty much the entire left side of her body and she felt so bad she didn't care that she was almost completely naked.

When she returned to bed she didn't know if she wanted the answer to the question but she asked it anyway. "What are you doing here? And in my robe," she added pulling the sheet up to cover her bare breasts.

Caroline sat back in the chair, gathering the front of the robe tight against her chest. She looked around the room as if searching for an escape route.

"We were worried about you. You took a nasty spill," she said weakly.

Shannon raised the glass to her mouth, her hand steadier than a moment ago. "I asked why *you* were here." Caroline's eyes darted around the room again before settling on her hands now clasped in her lap.

"I wanted to make sure you were all right. You needed some help getting into the tub...and...I..."

"Thank you," Shannon said quietly, ending Caroline's awkwardness. "I appreciate it. I don't know why, but I do appreciate it."

"It's what anyone would have done," Caroline said finally looking at her.

Shannon held her gaze, branding the clear cocoa color in her brain before she spoke again. "But nobody else did. Did they?"

Caroline stood, grabbed her clothes from the luggage rack, and disappeared into the bathroom. When she returned several minutes later, her hair was damp, her face freshly scrubbed. The bright blue jersey signifying her winning the previous race was smeared with dirt and sweat. Her bike shorts were tight and revealing and showed off her long muscular legs.

Shannon knew Caroline wasn't going to answer her question so she asked another instead. "Who won?"

"Gertrude Brasille over Stephanie McClennen. By eight tenths of a second." She buckled her shoes.

"What about you?" Shannon asked. Caroline held the second place slot when she left the starting gate.

"Third." Caroline didn't say anything else.

Shannon nodded her understanding and Caroline turned toward the door. She didn't want her to leave. "Where are you going?"

Caroline hesitated before turning back around. "You said yourself you're all right. I have to go. People are waiting for me."

Caroline didn't mention any names, but she didn't have to. Shannon had seen her and Fran together and she wondered what excuse she had given her girlfriend as to why she hadn't come home last night.

"Make sure she knows that I didn't take advantage of you in my weakened condition. Tell her I said thanks for sharing you."

Caroline's expression went from uncomfortable to confused to something Shannon couldn't quite put her finger on in the span of a few seconds as her words sank in. "Take care" was all Caroline said as she closed the hotel room door behind her.

Chapter Sixteen

"What are you doing?" Shannon flinched in surprise at the voice coming from behind her and was rewarded with sharp pain shooting through her left biceps. Most of her road rash was healed due to several days of intravenous antibiotics. The stitches were still a week away from removal, but all in all, three days after her fall she didn't feel too bad—considering. She concentrated on her movements as she took her bike out of the THS trailer, careful not to give any indication of her discomfort that would add fuel to the fire in Caroline's voice.

"Taking out my bike."

"Let me rephrase the question. What in the fuck are you doing?"

"Same answer."

"You're in no condition to race tomorrow." They were in Schladming, Austria, just east of Salzburg for the next to last race.

The nastiness combined with possessiveness made Shannon angry. "So in addition to getting a doctorate in, what was it again, astrophysics, you're now a physician?"

"Don't be flip." Caroline's eyes glowed with anger.

"Who do you think you are? You're not my mother or my girlfriend. Even if you were you wouldn't have any say in what I do or don't do."

"I wouldn't be your girlfriend for that and many other reasons. You wouldn't care what I thought, what I wanted, or if I were scared to death of what might happen to you."

"You're right on that one, honey. That's why I don't have a girlfriend. Because I don't care. I'm here to win the championship, not worry about what people think." Especially you, she thought.

Caroline shook her head. "You know, Shannon, if you do win, do you know what the caption will be under your picture? *Biker Babe Wins*. Better yet, you'll have some bike bimbo with big tits and no future draped all over you and you won't even remember her name, if you ever knew it to start with. You fuck anything that looks at you twice. You're more famous for the notches on your bike stem than what you do in the saddle." Caroline moved as Shannon rolled her bike to the side of the trailer but she didn't stop talking.

"You know I don't think people fundamentally change, but you're the exception. There is not one shred of the Shannon Roberts I knew. I don't know whether to pity you or envy you." Caroline did an about-face that any drill sergeant would be proud of. As she whirled, Shannon could practically feel the euphemistic slap on her face.

❖

Don't cry, don't cry, don't cry, Caroline chanted to herself. She was good at holding her emotions in check but nothing could stop the crack from forming in her heart—again. Tears burned behind her eyes and choked her throat. She had been so angry when she saw Shannon unloading her bike she had gone off the deep end.

It was a total surprise when she saw Shannon. The talk on the circuit and from the race sponsor was that Shannon would skip this week's race. Since the championship was won by the total number of points earned in the eleven races, the other riders were thrilled, believing this was their chance to gain valuable ground in the standing with their number one competitor out of the way—at least for this race. Caroline felt just the opposite. She was worried that Shannon was more seriously injured than she thought. After a day or two of worrying herself sick she finally talked herself into thinking that Shannon was sitting this one out because she didn't want to risk a more serious injury if she was not ready to compete.

She had seen how Shannon gingerly handled her bike and saw

how she was favoring her left arm and shoulder. The race this week was a single track course, the first half predominately uphill and scattered with rock and brush hanging over the track. The second half was all downhill with a series of switchback turns, some of which were 180 degrees over some of the roughest washboard trails on the series, made more dangerous due to the fatigue of the rider. One lapse of concentration or slip of a tire could mean disaster.

Caroline didn't remember exactly what she had said to Shannon, but the remnants of her anger still smoldered inside. She had seen Frank Striker's wife sniffing around Shannon and then when she gave every indication she was going to ride in a race she had no business riding in, it was too much for Caroline's taxed emotions.

She plastered on a smile when a man and woman approached asking for her autograph. He asked a few questions about her gear and bike but before Caroline had a chance to answer, his arm candy said, "Do you know Shannon Roberts? Have you seen her? Is she going to race this weekend? She is so hot in those tight shorts."

Her male friend jabbed her with his elbow and looked at Caroline as if to say "sorry" and looked embarrassed for both of them. Caroline simply nodded, too tired to say anything. He practically dragged the woman away from her, the questions about Shannon still spewing from her mouth. Several other race fans stopped and asked her questions or simply wanted a picture.

Don't cry, almost there, don't cry, almost there. Caroline screamed in her head approaching the elevator door. One, two, three, floor after floor she counted. Five, six, seven, eight steps to her door. She fished in her pockets for her door key. Where in the fuck is my key, she practically shouted, grateful for the empty hallway. She finally found it in her back pocket and inserted it into the lock. The green light flashed, the latch clicked, and when the door closed solidly behind her, Caroline fell to her knees and wept.

❖

Shannon watched Caroline walk away, stunned at the venom she heard in her voice. Who in the hell did she think she was, questioning

Shannon's decision to race this weekend? She was here to win the championship, not pussyfoot around over a few cuts and scrapes.

And what in the fuck did she say about the caption under my picture on the winner's stand? *Biker babe wins*? So what? It would be true. But that crack about the babe and the notches on her bike was a bit much. So what if the women she slept with didn't have a future? She wasn't looking for anything other than that night, maybe the next. She knew what she wanted out of life. She wanted to win.

What would Caroline's caption say? *Practice makes perfect*? Caroline was famous for her dedication to the sport. Shannon had a life and lived it every day. There was more to Shannon Roberts than training and riding. She had a life, and a very full one. What did Caroline have?

And what is with that bullshit that people don't change? She certainly had. Shannon was so deep in thought that her inspection of her bike and safety gear was more rote than real inspection. Caroline had graduated from Columbia University, one of the best colleges in the country, if not the world, not once but twice, with a degree in astrophysics. Shannon doubted she could spell it even with spell check. And she was going to be an astronaut. Shannon stopped suddenly, realizing exactly what Caroline had accomplished. But what had Shannon done?

Sure she had won races, lots of them. But what would her legacy be when she was done? And she would be done, and soon. The competition was getting younger and tougher. At eighteen, nineteen, or twenty, they were fearless and healed a lot faster. When would they start whispering behind her back, "She's embarrassing herself, she's too old, too slow, not as quick as she used to be. She doesn't have it anymore"?

Shannon didn't go to college. Hell, she barely finished high school because of the fiasco in Caroline's room. All she had wanted to do was ride. Even without a formal college education, she had done well for herself. She surrounded herself with people she trusted who knew what they were doing with the money she earned and her inheritance. She was financially set, and if she were careful, could probably do whatever she wanted for the rest of her life. But what would that be?

Shannon didn't like what she saw in her future. She didn't want to be a has-been that didn't know when to stop, when the competition had passed her by in the fast lane. She wanted to go out on top and she would do it this year, with this championship. Starting with this race, she would have no greater pleasure than beating the sanctimonious Caroline Davis.

CHAPTER SEVENTEEN

Ladies and gentlemen, riding for Bellow and wearing the blue leader's jersey, Caroline Davis." Even with her third place finish the race before, Caroline still led the series with the highest number of points.

Her concentration was so intense the only thing Caroline heard was the garbled muffle of her name being called. She didn't hear the roar of the crowd or the ring of the starter's bell but somehow knew when to shoot off the starting line.

Dig, dig, dig, she commanded her legs with each up and down stroke of the pedals. Stroke after stroke took her farther up the trail, her legs burning from exertion and her breathing heavy. Shifting eased some of the strain on her legs and she rose off the saddle, leaning over the handlebars for more traction and power.

Up, down, up, down, she commanded and before she knew it, she was at the top of the hill. Not sparing a moment to enjoy the view, she crested the trail and started her descent. Shift, shift, shift, shift, the popping of her gears was in direct synchronization with the up and down strokes of her thighs. Concentrate, easy, shift, brake, shift, pedal, hard turn, keep it tight, keep it tight, shift, pedal, pedal, were the commands in her head transferring to her body. Suddenly, she was out of the last turn and in the final straightaway. Dig, dig, dig, she chanted, this time out loud, and the roar of the crowd as she crossed the finish line drowned out any other sound. Skidding to a stop and breathing heavily, Caroline felt light-headed. Breathe in, out, in, out, she chanted in her head and her well-trained body followed directions. She had beaten everyone's time and the course record by an astonishing one point two seconds.

Her hands were shaking so badly she couldn't unbuckle her helmet strap. After a few moments, a familiar face was in front of her, and Fran's steady hands were doing the work for her.

"CD, you kicked ass, girl. If you keep this up, you'll wipe out the competition and have them for lunch."

Fran's all-access pass blew around her head in the breeze, almost poking Caroline in the eye.

❖

The knock on the door was unexpected. Caroline was in her robe. Normally she and Fran shared a room but Fran had insisted on her own this trip. Debating on whether or not to answer it, she stared at the door as if she could see through it. She sighed and got up when the knocking continued with no sign of stopping. She peered through the peephole and quickly stepped back as if it were blistering hot. In a way it was. Shannon was framed in the oblong lens looking right at her.

Caroline didn't know whether she was up to seeing Shannon. She was exhausted and, considering her reawakening feelings toward her, she knew she needed to be at her sharpest whenever she was with her. She didn't want to get caught up in the memory and say or do something she would regret later. Against her better judgment, she opened the door.

Caroline's stomach jumped when Shannon's face softened and she smiled. Her smile, with the slight dimple on her left cheek, had taken her breath away ten years ago and still had the same effect.

"I hope I'm not bothering you," Shannon said tentatively.

"No, not at all." Caroline closed the top of her nightgown when Shannon noticed the exposed flesh.

"I just wanted to…uh…compliment you on your ride today."

Shannon shifted her weight from foot to foot the way she used to when she was nervous.

"Thanks. I'm glad you're okay." That was the best she could do and even that was difficult. She was still pissed that Shannon had risked her life to race when she might not have been ready. She certainly wasn't going to congratulate her for doing something stupid.

It looked like Shannon wanted to say more and Caroline deliberated on whether or not to give her an opening. Silence hung in the air like fog before Shannon finally spoke.

"May I come in?"

A combination of excitement and uncertainty coursed through Caroline's body. What did she want? What else could she possibly have to say? A dozen other questions popped in her mind in the second it took her to make up her mind. Opening the door was just as much a signal for Shannon to come into the room as it was for her to step back into her life.

Shannon's hair smelled like strawberries again when she walked by and Caroline's hand shook as she closed the door. When she turned around Shannon was standing at the foot of the bed, looking at it as if it were going to swallow her. Caroline walked around her and opened the door to the minibar.

"Would you like something to drink?"

Shannon chuckled nervously. "I'd like a strong drink, but no thanks, I'm fine."

Watching Shannon's body language, Caroline knew she was anything but relaxed. She was wringing her hands, and her gaze shifted around the room before finally settling on Caroline. Shannon was making her nervous.

"Is there something on your mind?" Caroline wasn't sure if she wanted to know the answer to her question.

"Can we be friends?" Shannon asked softly in a rush of air.

Caroline wasn't sure if she heard her correctly. Could they be friends? Did she mean like hang out together, talk about their girlfriends, and go shopping?

"Are you fucking kidding?"

"I guess I am. You know me, the jokester?" This time her laugh was sarcastic and she stepped to the other side of the small room. "What ever would make me think you'd want to be civil with me? I must have hit my head harder than I thought I did when I fell. Maybe I should crash again. Maybe this time it'll knock some sense into me." The last sentence was directed more toward herself than Caroline.

The image of Shannon lying crumpled on the ground flashed in her eyes and her stomach dropped from where it was lodged in her throat to just above her crotch. "Don't say that, Shannon."

"Why not? It's obvious you don't want anything to do with me. You probably wish I'd hurt myself bad enough you could just coast to the winner's circle."

Shannon's eyes flashed in anger sparking Caroline's own answering furor. She marched the five steps to close the gap between them. "Don't you dare put words in my mouth." Caroline pointed her finger at Shannon. "You don't know the first thing about me. You don't know what I'm thinking. You have no idea what I want and you certainly can't speak for me." Caroline jabbed her finger into Shannon's chest emphasizing each point as she made it. When she was finished she was practically toe-to-toe with her.

"I know more about you than you do about yourself. I know what makes you tick. I know what buttons to push and levers to turn to make you crazy, and don't think I won't use them to my advantage." Shannon's breath was hot on her face. Her words felt like jagged shards of glass. The truth often hurt.

Shannon's eyes burned, this time with something very different. Something Caroline recognized immediately. Caroline forgot what she was going to say next. She was furious. Her heart was racing and her pulse beat in her brain. Before she knew what was happening, Shannon's lips were on hers.

Shannon couldn't control herself as she kissed Caroline. She was wound tight from pain, anger, and desire and she needed release. Holding Caroline's face between her hands, she devoured the mouth that could cause her such pain and unspeakable pleasure. Second after second, minute after minute, she kissed Caroline and Shannon had no idea when Caroline started kissing her back. She wanted more of her and the force of her kiss pushed Caroline against a small desk.

Shannon dropped her hands from Caroline's face to the belt of her robe, their lips never parting. The bare skin had teased her long enough and she easily untied the sash and slid her hands inside. When her hands met Caroline's soft skin again after so long, Shannon didn't even try to mask her moan of pleasure. Needing to feel every inch of her, Shannon slowly moved her fingers over Caroline's stomach, until finally cupping her breasts. Caroline leaned into her. That one little acknowledgment of Caroline's desire opened the floodgates of Shannon's pent-up desire along with the unending need to have her. To give Caroline every ounce of pleasure she possibly could. She was consumed by her.

Shannon spun them around and dragged Caroline's robe off leaving her naked in her arms. Her craving spiked as Caroline tugged and pulled on her clothes, and soon it was flesh against flesh, woman against woman on the big bed.

They fought for domination, until Shannon finally pinned Caroline's arms above her head. The throbbing in her injured leg had been replaced by throbbing between her legs and when Caroline slid her thigh between hers, Shannon fought for control.

As tempted as she was to fall into the orgasm that was pounding at the door, Shannon focused her attention on Caroline. She released Caroline's hands and trailed her mouth down Caroline's neck, planting hard, wet kisses along the way. Caroline grabbed the back of her head urging Shannon closer. Back and forth Shannon moved, kissing, sucking, and nibbling on Caroline's lips and exposed neck. It was a mating. The arch of Caroline's neck symbolic of an animal fully surrendering to its mate.

Shannon continued licking and sampling Caroline's skin with her tongue while her hands explored her womanly form. She was soft and warm, with curves and valleys in just the right places. Caroline's body was a wonderland years ago and she was going to rediscover every inch of it again.

Shannon felt Caroline's nipple grow harder in her palm. Her breast was larger than before, filling her hand with its soft suppleness. When she rolled the nipple between her fingers, lightly tugging on the hard tip, Caroline moaned softly. Caroline pushed her head downward in the universal symbol of need and when Shannon's mouth replaced her fingers, Caroline cried out in pleasure.

Shannon wanted to grind into the thigh moving between her legs to release the pressure that was building, waiting to explode. Instead, she shifted so that the temptation was not in direct contact with her hot flesh. She explored first one breast, then the other, taking her time to travel over every millimeter of soft, sensitive skin. As much as she was enjoying Caroline's breasts she needed to kiss her again, taste her lips, feel her tongue. To verify she was real. That this was actually happening. That Caroline was in her arms, not a willing substitute or the dream that had teased her for the past ten years.

Caroline's hands shook as they ran up and down her back. She clutched Shannon's ass and arched into her. Shannon knew she was ready. Ready to be touched, caressed, loved. With agonizing slowness, Shannon kissed her way down Caroline's tense, responsive body. Her hot kisses turned tender over the pale scar that ran down Caroline's leg, the dent in her knee, the brush burn on her calf.

It wasn't long before Shannon wanted, no needed, to taste Caroline again, smell her, see her beauty, but she also wanted to savor the anticipation. It felt like it was their first time together again. They were two very different women, who knew very little about each other. Discovering each other in a way they never had before. A thrill ran through Shannon as she remembered the sensations, the feelings of the times they were together before this moment. The moment just before she arrived at the center of her universe.

Caroline unabashedly spread her legs giving Shannon free access to her both literally and figuratively. Shannon's need increased more than she ever thought imaginable when her mouth touched Caroline's warm, wet center.

If she died right now, Shannon thought, she would die with everything she had ever wanted. She explored every curve, peak, and valley, discovering every hidden treasure within. She flicked her tongue over Caroline's clit. Caroline arched and grabbed the sheets in her fists and Shannon watched as she writhed in ecstasy. The vision was stunning. Caroline, lying naked with her. Her head thrown back, chest heaving with shallow breaths. Her entire body was moving. Every inch experiencing, receiving pleasure.

Caroline lifted her head, locking eyes with Shannon. At that moment, in that very instant, Shannon was connected to another human being like never before. She held their gaze and slowly stroked Caroline's clit with her tongue. She watched Caroline's eyes glaze as she increased the speed and pressure on the sensitive spot. Caroline's body moved in rhythm and Shannon knew she was very, very close to climax. She reached out grasping Caroline's hand as Caroline whispered her name and exploded in her mouth.

❖

The sun was just beginning to creep over the horizon when Shannon woke. Caroline was still sleeping, lying on her side with her head on Shannon's shoulder, her hand cupping one breast. Heat seared through Shannon's body as her mind flashed back to how they got here. What she and Caroline had shared through the night was breathtaking. Hour after hour they took turns pleasing each other, touching, kissing, stroking until finally falling asleep in complete exhaustion. The large clock on the nightstand read three forty-five just before she closed her eyes.

Today was a pivotal day in the series but Shannon didn't care. It was more important to be with Caroline, to talk to her, touch her, than it was to win the race. When Caroline whispered her name in the darkness, begged for relief, Shannon forgot about everything else.

Not wanting to wake her, Shannon gathered the clothes, picked up her shoes, and tiptoed toward the door. She dressed with as little movement as necessary so not to wake Caroline. Forgoing slipping into her shoes, Shannon tucked them under her arm and reached for the doorknob.

The click of the lock was deafening in the silence of the small room and she waited to see if the sound had woken Caroline. Hearing nothing, she turned the knob, opened the door, and took the first step into the hall. She was not prepared to come eye to eye with Steven Davis.

Shannon had seen that look before. It was the same one she saw in Caroline's doorway those many years ago. Confusion, shock, rage. But this time the circumstances were very different. Before, they were kids; today, grown women who had shared something magical that only adults can.

"Mr. Davis," she said firmly, knowing it wasn't really appropriate to say, "Good morning, Mr. Davis." By the look on his face, it was anything but. He didn't return the greeting but looked at her with fire in his eyes.

Shannon figured she had three choices. Go back in the room and close and lock the door, go around him, or stand her ground. She chose the last one. Contrary to the look on his face, Shannon wasn't concerned that he would hit her, no matter how much he may have wanted to.

They stared at each other as the seconds ticked by. Shannon swore she could hear the second hand on her watch move. She refused to back down. She had done that once and had regretted it almost every day after. She was an adult and demanded to be treated like one. She would stand there as long as she had to. She didn't have to wait long before Caroline's father finally spoke.

"It's my job to protect my daughter." His voice was barely controlled anger. "And I will do everything in my power to do so. I did it before and I'll do it again if I have to."

"Yes, sir, it is and she's very lucky to have you as her father."

"She was young and I did what I thought was best for her. I cut off any contact she had with you. Then you went to Switzerland and even if you were able to contact her at least you couldn't see her."

Davis continued and the pieces started to fall into place. That was why Caroline hadn't answered her phone and was so difficult to get in touch with. Her letters had been returned as well.

"I kept tabs on you for a few years. Made sure you stayed out of her life. You were committed to the European circuit, which at least put more than a few miles between you. When I was satisfied Caroline had forgotten about you and you her, I breathed easier. And now here you are. Again."

He took in her disheveled appearance and there was no doubt that Davis knew that "here" was in his daughter's bed. Shannon didn't take her eyes off his face.

"But Caroline was a child then and she's an adult now. She makes her own decisions. I may not agree with them, but she is my daughter and I support her." Shannon knew there was a but in there somewhere.

"But let me make one thing clear, Ms. Roberts. If you do anything to intentionally hurt Caroline, to cause her any pain whatsoever, you will answer to me."

Steven Davis had not raised his hand or his voice during the awkward conversation. He didn't have to. The love for his daughter was clear and Shannon had no doubt he would follow through on his actions. Before Shannon could reply, a sharp intake of breath came from over her left shoulder. Preparing for the worst, she turned and saw Caroline standing right behind her.

For the second time she watched the interaction between Caroline and her father. Like her father, Caroline's face showed shock, fear, and uncertainty. She was clutching her robe to her chest in a death grip, her knuckles white. Shannon watched Davis take in her just-fucked appearance and the fact that she was obviously very naked beneath the short silk robe. She wondered what it was like for a man to actually see his daughter as a sexual woman. Know what she had done, imagining someone touching her, stroking her, making her cry out in desire. In that instant, and that instant only, she felt sorry for him.

"I wouldn't expect anything less from you, Mr. Davis," Shannon said. She turned and faced Caroline. As much as she wanted to, there was nothing she could do to help her. This was between Caroline and her father. She reached out, grasped Caroline's hand for a moment, and smiled what she hoped was a sign conveying that she was with her before stepping around her father.

"Daddy," Caroline said, not knowing what to say. Her father entered the room, the two cups of coffee he was holding all but forgotten. Caroline glanced at Shannon's retreating back before closing the door.

"What you do is your business, Caroline. It's not my place to interfere like it was years ago. I did what I thought was necessary and I'd do it all again if I had to. But you're a grown woman now with a smart head on her shoulders. You make your own decisions and I support you. You're my daughter and I love you. Nothing will ever change that. Now, let's get you ready for the race today, shall we?"

Caroline stood there speechless. She certainly hadn't expected to see her father and Shannon together this morning. God, especially not *this* morning. The sound of voices woke her and when she saw who was talking and heard what they were saying, she was practically paralyzed in the past. Shannon was standing her ground with her father and he was making his intentions clear. What may have looked like a stalemate to others was really a meeting of the minds of two of the most important people in her life. After a moment, she padded over to her father in her bare feet and lightly kissed him on the cheek.

❖

Shannon was oblivious to the activity around her as she walked the short distance down the hall to the waiting elevator. It was empty, thank God. She didn't feel like she could make small talk with anyone she knew. She looked at her reflection in the mirror. Her eyes were tired but bright, her face flushed. Did she look any different than she had when she exited this same elevator hours ago? She certainly felt different.

Sometime last night with Caroline she had changed. In the minutes before dawn, Shannon had thought not only about what had happened between them, but how it had affected her. She had touched and been touched. Not just physically, but emotionally, and it frightened her. She had never felt this way about anyone, never allowed herself to. The more she thought about it, the more she realized that no one had ever taken the place of Caroline. No one had even come close. For lack of any other way of describing it, she felt like she had come home.

Shannon unlocked the door with the cardkey she pulled from her pocket and stepped inside. The strength of the early morning light barely penetrated the drawn drapes. She let her shoes drop on the floor and lay on her own queen size bed. She curled up in a ball wanting to savor and remember the taste, the touch, the feel, the scent of Caroline Davis.

The smell of her was still on her fingers, the taste of her in her mouth. Shannon didn't care how ridiculous she appeared as she licked one finger after the other, inhaling the scent of the woman who meant the world to her. They hadn't talked much during the night. They hadn't talked about anything at all. They simply reached out to each other time and time again; their need for each other unspoken. Words would trivialize what they were experiencing. Shannon had never felt so loved and felt so much love for someone in return. What she had felt for Caroline before was simply young love. What she sensed now was the full, mature love of one woman for another. She savored the feeling for one more moment before getting up, peeling off her clothes, and stepping into the shower.

CHAPTER EIGHTEEN

Shannon was next on the starting line. The final of this race was a series of three heats. She and Caroline had both completed the first two and Caroline was ahead of her by eight tenths of a second. This was her final run. Shannon had to ride her best to give herself enough cushion so that Caroline had to ride better to beat her.

The start clock ticked down and Shannon readied herself for the most important race of the series so far. She had pushed Caroline out of her mind as soon as she had turned off the shower faucet knobs. She had to focus. She couldn't allow Caroline to intrude on her concentration.

Five, four, three, two, one. Shannon rocketed out of the starting blocks. Her skill and strength climbing hills dominated the tour and she had no trouble on the first half of the race. Up and down her powerful legs moved, each stroke of the pedals churning over the dirt effortlessly under her wheels. Her ass was out of the saddle giving the extra power she needed to get over the next rise. Crossing the top, she immediately downshifted and tried to make up any speed she might lose on the downhill side of the course.

Alternating shifting and pedaling down the hill, stroke after stroke, her full face helmet and goggles kept any wind off her face. The bandana under her helmet kept the sweat from dripping into her eyes. Her long sleeves rustled in the breeze created by her fast descent.

A sharp turn came quicker than expected, and her disc brakes responded immediately to the command to slow down. She mastered the turn without the slightest hesitation and was pedaling even before she was out of the turn. She repeated these movements time and time again, turn after hairpin turn, as she steadily descended the mountain. She crossed the finish line with a time of 5:22:04. She glanced behind her knowing that her main rival and the woman who had come back into her life was preparing herself at the start line at that very moment.

Shannon walked over to the post-race staging area to watch Caroline on the JumboTron. Due to the wonders of modern technology, Shannon could watch the entire race, and as the seconds ticked down to zero, Caroline jetted out of the starting gate.

Caroline climbed the steep ascent. She was a woman in control of the mountain, her tires on her lime green bike kicking up no dust as they churned up the steep trail. Her arms were as powerful as her legs and Shannon watched in awe as she used them to give herself extra leverage and power to climb the hill.

On the back side of the mountain Caroline practically floated over the steep terrain. She mastered each turn, one after the other, almost effortlessly, but the fatigue in Shannon's arms and legs told her that even though Caroline made it look easy, it was anything but. Shannon held her breath as Caroline maneuvered through each turn, knowing that any minor slip and Caroline could go down as hard as she had the week before.

Finally, Caroline was through the last turn and Shannon dragged her eyes away from the screen to watch her speed to the finish. Caroline flashed by the banners on either side of the straightaway as she came closer and closer to the checkered flag. Twenty yards, fifteen yards, ten, five. With a flash and a roar Caroline crossed the line.

The crowd erupted and Shannon had no indication if she had won or lost this race. She was afraid to look at the scoreboard where the time of all three races was displayed. She wanted to win. She wanted to show Caroline that she knew what was best for her, that she could still compete even with a few bumps and bruises. But a piece of her also wanted Caroline to have some of the glory as well. Caroline had worked hard, had trained diligently for this, and a small part of Shannon wanted it for her.

She had won dozens and dozens of races. Big ones, big-name races, races that had catapulted her to the top of the heap, and her skill kept her there for years. Caroline had also won her share of races, some larger and more important than others. But what came naturally to Shannon she knew Caroline had to work and struggle and sacrifice to achieve. And Shannon admired her for that. It was one thing to win something that comes easily, but another to struggle and work and put your heart and soul into something that you may or may not win.

All these thoughts crashed through Shannon's head in the span of the second it took her to look up from Caroline crossing the line to the scoreboard. She had beaten Caroline by three tenths of a second.

The crowd swarmed her slapping her on the back, the top of her helmet, her ass, with quite a few idiots slapping her on her injured arm. She was grateful for the protective gear. She had learned early on, albeit the hard way, that race fans had a tendency to be overexuberant in their congratulatory wishes.

Shannon fought to look through the crowd to catch a glimpse of Caroline. She saw her. She had not yet dismounted, her forearms dangling over the handlebars, her head down in defeat. It was late in the afternoon on Sunday and Caroline was silhouetted in the sun making her disappointment more poignant. Shannon watched Fran approach Caroline and give her a very conciliatory, sympathetic hug. Shannon's mind went down an ugly trail that Fran would find a way later tonight to boost Caroline's spirits.

A sick feeling in the pit of her stomach came with the knowledge that Caroline was the type of woman who would sleep with one woman one night and a different one the next. She didn't know why she was upset with that; she had done it many times herself. But it was different with Caroline. Or at least her gut told her it should be. Caroline hadn't said anything about a girlfriend, but then again, it wasn't as if they had stopped fucking long enough to have a conversation. The only things they said to each other last night were words like "yes," "right there," "faster," "harder," "again," and several others that two people having sex would share. A flash of anger shot through her limbs, her arms flailing and almost knocking a few fans to the ground. She mumbled something akin to an apology and used her bike to clear a path through the crowd.

She knew she would be seeing Caroline on the winner's platform, Shannon on the top step, Caroline on the step reserved for the second place finisher. Caroline would remove the blue leader jersey before stepping on her box, and after receiving her own medal, Shannon, now ahead in the standing by a mere three points, would receive her own blue jersey that she would be wearing in next week's race. Shannon despised baby blue; it made her look pale and washed out. She thought it a sissy color, but she would accept it nonetheless.

As Shannon removed her helmet, strong female hands grabbed her shoulders, spun her around, and pinned her in a lip lock. She had no idea who it was other than a woman who was trying to stick her tongue down her throat. As respectfully and calmly as she could, Shannon pushed her away. When she saw who it was she wanted to gag.

Forcing herself not to spit out the evidence of Nikki Striker's kiss, Shannon plastered a fake smile on her face and waved at the crowd who were cheering as if she had just kissed the most beautiful woman in the world. She kept her grip on Nikki, squeezing her arm tight, conveying her disapproval of her actions. She was furious with Nikki for taking advantage of her and putting her in this position. But she knew the role she had to play and at this very moment in her biking career, she was sick of it. Frank approached from her right slapping her on the back so hard it was all she could do not to gasp for air to refill her lungs.

"That's my girl. I knew you could beat her. I knew. There was never any doubt. You got the brains and the look and the skill. You're gonna take this whole goddamn thing. You're going to clean fucking up. Nobody has what you have. And you're mine, all mine."

Shannon broke away from Frank more roughly than she had his wife. She wasn't going to put up with his shit. Not today. She was tired, she hurt everywhere, her arm was killing her, and it felt like her stitches on her leg had pulled out. To top it all off, his sleazy wife had blindsided her with probably the most disgusting kiss in her life. The last two minutes had spoiled her win. To the winners go the spoils, and if Nikki and Frank Striker were the spoils, she had to rethink her goals in life.

CHAPTER NINETEEN

Caroline watched in dismay as Shannon was surrounded by her sponsor and a woman who could only be Nikki Striker. There were rumors on the circuit about Nikki, and she chose not to believe them. She didn't believe the chatter on the circuit because half the rumors were false, and it was often only a matter of time before the other half became true. And quite frankly, she didn't care if they were about her and she certainly didn't care if they were about the woman who had snatched the victory right out from under her tires. No, that wasn't fair. She didn't slip, didn't make any errors. She had run this course perfectly. Shannon had beaten her fair and square and she gave her her due. In this race, Shannon was the more skilled rider. She had won this race, not stolen it from her, and Caroline had not given it to her. Shannon had beaten her. Caroline's head knew that, but her heart and stomach felt just the opposite.

"You all right?" Fran's familiar voice calmed her jittery nerves.

She was in the Bellow trailer alone, shooing everyone out. She needed her privacy, she needed a moment, she needed to regroup, she needed to prepare herself to remove the blue jersey and hand it over to Shannon Roberts. Fran was one of the few people she was willing to see in these moments. She knew what to say and, most importantly, what not to say. There were no empty words of platitude. No you'll get it next time. She didn't say anything to her. Fran knew her. Knew what Caroline needed probably better than she knew herself. She needed just a friendly face, a calming smile, and the presence of her very best friend.

Caroline shed the jersey, folding it neatly before setting it on the table beside her. Clad only in her T-shirt, sports bra, and body armor, she loosened the laces on the hard plastic chest protector. Without thinking, she peeled off her T-shirt and her sports bra, unconcerned of her nakedness in front of Fran. They had seen each other naked before, either in the gym, skinny-dipping, or in situations just like this. They were friends, nothing more. She didn't think twice about it and neither did Fran.

"What in the hell is that?" Fran asked in her not-so-subtle way.

"What?" It took a moment for Caroline to register what Fran was talking about. When it dawned on her that she was staring at her breast she remembered that there was a vivid reminder of the passionate sex she had shared with Shannon the night before. She felt her face flush with embarrassment. Wasn't it she who made a disparaging comment about Shannon's hickey that night weeks ago?

"Exactly what it looks like," Caroline replied, knowing the twenty questions had just begun.

"I know what it is. Where did you get it?"

"Right here on my left breast," Caroline countered in an attempt to joke her way out of an awkward situation.

"That's not what I meant and you know it. Give." Fran waved her fingers at Caroline.

"Fran, I don't want to—"

"Details, Davis. What happened last night after we left?" She held up her hand, palm facing Caroline. "Wait, don't answer that. I don't want a smart-ass answer. *Who* gave that to you?" She pointed at the red bruise for effect.

Caroline didn't want to share the night she had spent with Shannon with anyone. She was still processing exactly what had happened, or more specifically how she had let it happen. Again and again, as a matter of fact. The butterflies in her stomach started up again. She had felt jittery ever since waking up this morning to find Shannon and her father in the doorway. But she also knew Fran would not let up until she had all the answers.

"Shannon." Caroline braced herself for the onslaught that would come. Fran didn't disappoint her.

"Shannon? As in my red hot high school lover that my dad caught me with Shannon?" Fran always did have a way with words.

"Yes, and I don't want to talk about it." She grabbed the clothes Fran had removed from the locker at the far end of the trailer. Caroline went to the basin, drew some water and a washcloth, and quickly washed her face, arms, and neck, splashing some of the cool liquid over her head.

"Too bad. You're not getting away that easily."

Caroline pulled on a fresh T-shirt with Bellow broadcast across her chest in bright yellow letters against the black background. "Fran, please. I can't." Her voice cracked on the last two words. Caroline took another quick look at herself in the mirror, checking to make sure she didn't have any dirt on her face. She grabbed another full bottle of Gatorade and stepped out the door.

Shannon watched Caroline approach the winner's stand holding her head high. She was proud of her accomplishment, and Shannon was proud of her. Caroline received several congratulatory hugs, handshakes, and even a few kisses. As her name was called, she stepped onto the platform, a smile on her face that Shannon thought didn't quite reach her eyes. But anyone that didn't know her as well as she did wouldn't know the difference. She lifted her arms in the air and waved at the crowd showing her appreciation for their cheers. She stepped up onto the box and the crowd roared again. Caroline acknowledged them with another wave and a dip of her head, which was true Caroline Davis style. She was a gracious winner and a more gracious loser. She never said anything negative about her fellow racers; she recognized their skill and their accomplishments and simply moved on to the next competition.

The mayor of Schladming presented Caroline with a bouquet of flowers and draped the second place medal over her head and it bounced lightly against her chest. He shook her hand and kissed both cheeks in the European way and stepped aside.

Shannon knew she was next. She wanted to let Caroline savor this moment, but this was her race. She had won, damn it. Against all odds, she had shown them, all of them. Especially Caroline. As she approached the winner's platform her eyes never left Caroline's.

She tried desperately to read what was in those dark eyes but she couldn't. One second they said, "great race," the next, "you could have goddamned killed yourself." It didn't really matter. It was over. It was done. And as she stepped up on the highest position on the platform, the only thing she cared about was how good it felt to be on top.

She turned to her left, shaking the hand of the third place winner. She turned to her right and when her hand touched Caroline's it was as if a jolt of electricity went from her fingertips to her feet, practically gluing her to the platform. For a few seconds she couldn't move. She couldn't breathe. She couldn't do anything but look into the smoldering eyes looking up at her. There was a connection between them. There always had been and even after ten years it was still there. Shannon didn't know whether to be thrilled or scared to death.

The festivities over, the photographs began. Snap after snap, flash after flash, all vying to get the perfect shot. One persistent writer followed Shannon back to the TKS trailer. He bombarded her with questions the entire way.

"So, Shannon, how do you feel? Did your injuries slow you down at all? Did your injury compromise your chance to win the race? Did you feel any different out there? Were you afraid to go down the mountain? Were you afraid you were going to fall again? What was going through your mind at the top of the hill? Do you have any kind of post-traumatic stress syndrome from your fall?"

The reporter and his asinine questions dogged her the hundred yards to her trailer. Shannon kept her temper, knowing that he could easily paint a very ugly picture of her in his article with the simple tap of the keys.

She was polite but clearly brushed him off when she got to the door. She stepped inside and the coolness of the air conditioner chilled the sweat on her skin. Unfortunately, she wasn't alone.

"Well, the champion has finally arrived," a not so sultry voice greeted her. Shannon thought for a moment to step outside into the clutches of the idiot reporter.

"Nikki." Shannon knew Nikki expected her to cross the trailer to her locker, but there was no way that was going to happen. It was too far away from the door and too close to Nikki.

"I just wanted to offer my congratulations."

Nikki's tone immediately told Shannon that she was after more than a simple acknowledgment of a job well done.

"Thanks," Shannon replied, trying to keep it light while at the same time surveying her options—they were few.

Nikki walked across the floor, her eyes pinning Shannon with a look that said this time she was going to get what she wanted. Shannon's mouth went dry but it was not due to desire.

"Nikki," she said.

"Shannon, you look a little tense. You were awesome out there. The way you handled that bike gave me the shivers. You were one with it. It was as if it was an extension of you. The way you handled that mountain was how you would make love to a woman. Strong, demanding, unrelenting."

Shannon almost choked at the absolute ridiculousness of what she was hearing. How could anyone equate what she had just done, what she had to do, what she put her body through, to making love to a woman? She never conquered a woman; she never needed to.

"I've never heard it phrased quite that way."

"You've never had anyone watch you like I've been watching you."

"I'm sure Frank appreciates you keeping an eye on me." She had no idea why she injected his name into the conversation. Nikki was immune to it; it meant nothing to her. Nothing was going to stop her. She wasn't getting the hint. Subtlety was not working with this woman. And that was exactly what Shannon was afraid of.

"Frank has no idea how I've been watching you."

Before Shannon had a chance to respond Nikki had her in a second unwanted lip lock pushing her against the lockers. She had her tongue in her mouth and her hands up her shirt before Shannon even realized it. Shannon tried to squirm away from her, but Nikki was stronger than she looked. Shannon had to use more force than she thought she would. She was breathing heavily from anger but not nearly as heavily as Nikki was from desire.

"Nikki." Shannon seemed to be repeating herself and getting nowhere.

"You want this as much as I do. Frank doesn't know and if he did he wouldn't care. All he's interested in is your body for the money it can make him." She moved closer to Shannon again. "I, on the other hand, am also interested in your body but for what it can do for me, and what I can do for you. I know your type, what you want. Quick, fast, anonymous. Let's celebrate your victory."

"That's very flattering, Nikki, but I've told you, and at the risk of pissing you off, I'm going to repeat myself. I don't do this. I don't do married women. I don't do straight women, and I certainly don't do the boss's wife."

The look in Nikki's eyes told Shannon that she was trying to decide if she was going to get angry or let it pass and try again. She chose the former.

"Who do you think you are?" she spat. "Where in the hell do you think you'd be without my Frank and his company? Who gives you money, buys your first class tickets, your hotel suites? You ride a bike, a silly little bike. One that happens to cost eight thousand dollars. For a bicycle, for God's sake. How stupid is that? You would have nothing if not for my husband. And you are very close to having nothing again."

Nikki was not known for her subtlety, and she didn't disappoint Shannon now. There was no mistaking the innuendo in her words. With one word to her husband, she could have Shannon's contract canceled. She would do it.

"Nikki, I'm sorry if I offended you. You're a very attractive woman. Another place, another time, another situation." Shannon let the words hang in the air letting Nikki draw her own conclusions. "But I don't do this. I'm sorry if it upset you."

"Don't flatter yourself," Nikki snapped. "I can have any women here I want. As a matter of fact, I have. And your main competitor, I've seen the way she looks at me. I think I'll go over to her trailer and see how she's doing. See if she needs any consoling from her loss." Without another word she spun and left with a parting, "Ta ta."

❖

Caroline felt it was only right to congratulate Shannon. She had run a good race. She looked around the expo grounds and the vendors packing up their wares. With no sign of Shannon, she headed to the

TKS trailer. It would be the last place she'd look before going back to her hotel room.

Caroline didn't knock on the door. She didn't think she needed to. She didn't think at all. She opened the door and froze. Shannon was pressed up against the lockers, a woman's body flush against her hers. From the angle, Caroline couldn't see who it was, but she was able to see it was a serious kiss and the woman's hands were under Shannon's shirt, palms splayed across her breasts.

They were obviously too deep in what they were doing to notice that she had walked into the tête-à-tête. Finding Shannon in such a compromising position was shocking. Caroline backed out as silently as she entered.

"Stupid, stupid, stupid." She berated herself with each step taking her farther away from the scene that was burned into her mind. Why did it bother her so much? Shannon was a playgirl, she knew it. She had accused her of it earlier and Shannon hadn't said anything to try to change her mind. So why should she be so upset to find her in such a position? She had no claims on her. Shannon had said as much to her earlier. Why shouldn't she celebrate her victory in any way she wanted? Hell, if I'd won the race and had a good-looking woman, I'd be celebrating the same way as well. But this was different. This was Shannon and she had made love to her not twelve hours ago.

Since they'd made contact again, she thought about Shannon constantly. Why couldn't she get her out of her mind? It was obvious that Shannon was no good for her. She didn't even want her. Caroline didn't want Shannon in her life. She had a career, a future. NASA was waiting. Shannon was a career liability and Caroline knew it. She couldn't risk it. She wouldn't risk it. Shannon had no place in her life. Could she imagine showing up at a NASA party with Shannon on her arm? She might as well give up her dream of being an astronaut right now. It would never happen.

She came to see Shannon and what did she get? A slap in the face—again. She was much better off when they weren't speaking to each other. Barely acknowledging each other's existence. There was a lot less pain and confusion the way it used to be. She walked back to her hotel room vowing Shannon would never hurt her again.

CHAPTER TWENTY

The flight to Melbourne for the final race of the series was grueling. The fact that Fran peppered her with questions about her night with Shannon didn't help.

When she had an opportunity to close her eyes, all Caroline saw was images of Shannon. The fire in her eyes just before she kissed her. The trembling of her hands as she removed her clothes. The hard, demanding kisses of desire. Shannon wanted her and Caroline had surrendered without a second thought. Jesus, what had she been thinking? Shannon was her rival. She stood in the way of everything Caroline wanted, what she had trained for, sacrificed for. She could not afford the diversion and disruption Shannon caused in her life. Not now. Not when she was so close to winning.

But she had. Boy had she. Heat raced through her body as it reflexively recalled Shannon's touch. How she had practically begged for her touch. Caroline wasn't normally an overly aggressive lover, but with Shannon she was insatiable. The instant Shannon's lips touched hers she lost everything. Her inhibition, her doubts, fears, and most troubling, herself.

Making love with Shannon was the most exciting, most moving experience of her life. It was nothing in comparison to what they had shared years ago and absolutely nothing like the women she had been with since. It was more than simply the physical release. Her heart pounded in her chest, her blood churned, and she was lost in sensation and emotion. Shannon's lips were soft, her tongue teasing, her hands in her hair holding Caroline to her while she flicked her tongue over Shannon's hard clit. She wanted Shannon. She halfheartedly tried to tell herself that it just happened, that Shannon had taken advantage of her. But that was bullshit. She knew what she was doing from the moment it started, and she did nothing to stop it. She didn't want to.

No one made her body respond the way it did when Shannon touched her. No one excited her with just a look. No one made her come alive like Shannon did. She had never compared lovers, but now that she had been with Shannon again Caroline realized that no one could ever compare.

But it would never happen again. Not after seeing Shannon and the woman yesterday. The woman's hands were under Shannon's shirt and it appeared as though both of them were getting what they wanted. She hadn't stayed around to see the rest, preferring to throw up in private behind the trailer instead.

Caroline eventually made it through customs and to the cool hotel room in Canberra. With a population of over 345,000, Canberra was Australia's eighth largest city, located 170 miles southwest of Sydney and 410 miles northeast of Melbourne. The race was to be held at Stratford Park with over twenty-five miles of fire trail and single track trails.

The twenty-four hours of Australia was a grueling marathon of riding through some of the most breathtaking, treacherous terrain on the continent. After ten races in twelve weeks, the course pitted rider against nature against the clock against stamina. The race was simple. The rider who completed the most laps in the twenty-four-hour period won.

The race began with the riders running four hundred yards to their bikes. Once they were in the saddle, a three-mile fire trail ascended the mountain before the course turned to seven miles of twisting, turning single track before another three miles of flat trail led back to the starting point. Each rider was fitted with a GPS so that race officials knew exactly where every rider was at all times. The round trip was thirteen miles, providing the riders plenty of time to spread out the pack.

In the eight years the event had been held at the park, no rider, male or female, had ridden the course for the entire twenty-four hours. Riders were able to stop and start at their leisure, riding as many laps as they could with any number of rest breaks in between. There were no limitations.

The race started at four p.m. Last year, due to her injury, Caroline was unable to compete at full throttle throughout this race. She finished fifty-sixth. Respectable, considering her injury, but it was a heartbreaking finish nonetheless. This year Caroline knew how she was going to attack the course. She was going to complete five laps then take a ten-minute break. She would repeat this sequence for the first three hours then increase her break time by five minutes in each sequential three-hour block. The race was similar to a marathon in which runners ran 26.2 miles. The first half of the race, generally speaking, was pretty easy for most runners. It was the second half that was more difficult, and the seasoned runners knew that it was the last six miles that made the difference between winning the race or not.

The terrain was a combination of dirt, sand, rocks, pea gravel, boulders, and washboard roads that would rattle the fillings out of any unsuspecting rider's teeth. It wasn't unheard of that after the first ten hours of the race, half of the contestants had either voluntarily withdrawn or involuntarily withdrawn due to a fall or a mechanical breakdown they couldn't repair. When the mental and physical fatigue set in was when mistakes began. Hands went numb from their tenuous grip on the handlebars. Fingers started to blister from the constant pressure from squeezing the brake levers. Toes tingled from the continuing pressure of pushing down on the pedals. Leg muscles quivered from the sliding back in the saddle on the descent, pushing on the ascent, and absorbing all the shock on the way down.

If the riders didn't rest, rehydrate, and refuel they would find themselves in the dirt. Sometimes they would be able to pick themselves up and continue, but more often than not, they would be seriously injured with a broken arm, broken collarbone, or worse. Caroline knew that this would be a test not only of her physical stamina but of her mental stamina as well.

❖

Caroline had intentionally kept an eye out for Shannon in the airport, hotel lobby, and here in Canberra. She knew she couldn't avoid her for long, but the longer she did delayed the inevitable.

She felt like a fool, or an idiot. She wasn't sure which. How stupid of her to think that Shannon wanted something from her other than a quickie trip down memory lane. The sex between them had always been more than unbelievable.

The scene with Shannon and her father two mornings ago was still fresh in her mind. She needed to put it in its proper place and devote her full concentration on preparing for this race. The races in this series had been won and lost in tenths of a second. This race would be determined by much more than that.

❖

Shannon finally cornered Caroline three days later. She had knocked on Caroline's hotel door until her knuckles bled, staked out the practice runs, and roamed the park grounds desperately searching for her. It was as if she had not arrived, but Shannon knew better. The Bellow trailer was there and showed signs of constant activity. But no matter what she did, or where she went, she was never able to connect with Caroline.

She wanted to see Caroline again. Needed to see her again. Shannon had to reinforce the connection they shared because it didn't seem real. She thought she didn't have any residual feelings for Caroline, but one touch, one kiss, and she knew she had been lying to herself all these years. The feelings intensified as she finally saw Caroline walking across the expo grounds.

Shannon slipped behind the giant tent to cut off Caroline's access to her sponsor trailer. She stepped out from behind a stack of boxes and gently grabbed Caroline's hand and pulled her back into the area away from the prying eyes of others. Before Caroline had a chance to react, Shannon covered her mouth in a searing kiss. Shannon's head spun from the contact and she was left hanging when Caroline pushed her away.

"Don't touch me." Caroline's voice was harsh.

"What?" Shannon was dizzy from the kiss and Caroline's rejection. She hadn't expected this reaction.

"You heard me." Her voice was like ice.

"What are you talking about?"

"You know damn good and well what I'm talking about. If you think for one minute I'm going to stand for that, to be treated like another one of your biker babes, you have another think coming. Get out of my way."

Caroline started to brush by but Shannon grabbed her arm and stopped her. She had no idea what Caroline was talking about and was not going to let her walk away again. Before she had the chance to say anything else, Caroline slapped her. Hard.

"I said don't touch me." Shannon had never seen such flames of anger in Caroline's eyes. "Not after her. Now get out of my way." Caroline enunciated each word. Shannon was too stunned to do anything but let her walk away.

Frowning, Shannon shook her head trying to clear it. What in the hell just happened? What was Caroline talking about? Her who? Those and several other questions pounded in her head as she walked back in the direction she had just come. With each step Shannon relived every moment after their night together searching for something, anything, that would give her a clue to what Caroline was talking about.

Shannon stopped suddenly and her stomach lurched, pushing bile into her throat. Nikki. It had to be. Somehow, Caroline must have seen Nikki with her and assumed the worst. It couldn't be anything other than that. She had barely spoken to anyone after the race, and certainly not in a way that would lead Caroline to believe she had been with anyone else. She pivoted and ran after Caroline.

"Caroline, wait. It's not what you're thinking," Shannon shouted when she was still yards away from her retreating form. "Caroline, let me explain," she added finally alongside, hurrying to keep up with Caroline.

Caroline didn't respond or even acknowledge that she knew Shannon was at her elbow. "Caroline, please." She was not above begging. Caroline stopped so suddenly Shannon ended three steps ahead of her.

"Let me make this perfectly clear. Leave me alone. Don't talk to me, try to see me, or even look at me. That night was a mistake. A very bad mistake. And it will *never* happen again." Caroline walked away leaving Shannon breathless with fear.

CHAPTER TWENTY-ONE

But this time she did something about it. Caroline hadn't gone five yards before Shannon caught up with her and blocked her retreat.

"I don't know what in the hell you think you saw, but you're going to listen to what I have to say." Her feet were planted firmly in front of Caroline and there was no way she was getting around her. When Caroline tried, Shannon shuffled her feet to maintain her position.

"I don't give a shit what you have to say," Caroline growled.

"And I don't care what you think," Shannon shot back. This did little to deflate Caroline's anger and she crossed her arms in front of her in typical defensive body language, her face devoid of any emotion. Shannon was not going to be deterred.

"I ran away from you once before, and it's not your turn to do it to me. Not like this. There is nothing going on between me and Nikki Striker. There never has been and there never will be. She's been after me forever, but I am not interested and I've told her that on more than one occasion. What you saw was just another attempt to get me…her way of trying to convince me…to get me to change my mind…" Shannon was flustered, unable to find the right words. The right words were important. She needed to convince Caroline that Nikki was nothing, never was, and never would be.

"You don't expect me to believe that you turned her down? She's just your type."

Caroline's words stung, but then again the truth sometimes did.

With her reputation, why should Caroline believe her? She had to make her believe it.

"Yes, Caroline, I do expect you to believe me." Caroline's amused expression said it all. "And let me tell you why. First, I've never lied to you. Never. Well, there was that one time when you found that locket in my drawer and I told you it was for my mother," Shannon said trying a little humor to deflect her nerves. It didn't work.

"Seriously, Caroline. I didn't lie to you when we were together, and I'm not lying to you now. If I'd slept with half the women I've been rumored to, I wouldn't be here. You know what it takes to compete at this level."

Caroline's body had not relaxed but she wasn't trying to sidestep her anymore either.

"I've missed you. I didn't realize how much until the other night. And no, it's not about sex," she added hastily lest Caroline think it was all about the sex. "I miss talking to you, holding you, watching you move, listening to you breathe, seeing the sparkle in your eyes when you're excited, the fire when you're angry. I miss arguing with you, debating with you, agreeing with you."

Shannon took a chance that Caroline wouldn't run and stepped away a foot or two. She needed to move, to help herself think. The words were pouring through her and threatened to spill out of her mouth unchecked.

"I'm sorry I left you all those years ago. I was a stupid kid who didn't know any better. I was afraid. Afraid of my feelings for you. Scared to death of your father. Dean Phillips held my future in her hands. Without you I didn't have anybody to lean on, nobody to help me get through it. My parents were only concerned with themselves. They had no clue how to be parents. I let you go and spent years trying to find your replacement. But I never did because no one can ever take your place in my heart, in my life. I never should have let you go without tracking you down to the ends of the earth." Shannon took a breath, her courage building.

"I've done some things in my life I'm not terribly proud of. Especially after…well, after high school. I'm not going to make any excuses or try to pretend they didn't happen. I was ugly and mistreated people and I can't begin to say how sorry I am. If I could make it up in some way, I would. But all I can do right now is accept it, learn from it, and try to be a better person because of it."

Shannon was suddenly very tired, like she'd been carrying a heavy wet blanket around her shoulders for the past ten years. She was weary and worn out, fatigue pulling down her limbs and her spirit. She had one more thing to say and she had to get it right. She might never have another opportunity.

"I wish I could do it all over again, that day. I'd tell your father that I loved you and I wanted us to be together for the rest of our lives. I'd tell him that he might be able to keep us apart until we were eighteen but after that, we'd be adults and would be together regardless of what he said. I'd tell him that I'd take care of you, in sickness and in health, for better or worse, and all the other words people in love say when they make a commitment to each other. And I would forsake all others. I'd say all that, Caroline, because I loved you."

Shannon stopped pacing and stood directly in front of Caroline. Risking painful rejection, she grasped Caroline's hands in hers. She felt them shaking. "And I'd say it all again today because I still love you. I've never stopped loving you; I just didn't know it. But I do now and I will do anything to convince you of it. Whatever you want me to do or say I will. I don't want to lose you again."

Shannon was breathing fast. She took the first deep breath in minutes and tried to calm her racing nerves. She had no idea she was going to say what she had, but realized that it was the truth. Every single word. She had used other women to try to find the same thrill, excitement, and connection she had had with Caroline. The more she failed, the more she tried until being with Caroline again ended the spiral.

Shannon expected Caroline to say something, anything. But she just stood where she was and stared at her, her expression unreadable. Shannon didn't know whether to repeat everything she'd just said or fall on her knees and beg. She'd do anything to see Caroline smile at her, reach for her, touch her again. But she didn't. Caroline simply walked away. Again. This time Shannon let her go.

❖

Caroline readied herself at the starting line. Glancing around, she recognized the faces she had seen for the past three months. Some looked tired and haggard, others deep in concentration, and no one was smiling and joking like they were before the first race. It seemed like a lifetime ago and when it came to what had happened with Shannon, it was.

She had managed to avoid Shannon for the past four days. When she did catch a glimpse of her on the track or on the expo grounds, Caroline changed her course so as not to run into her. Her voicemail was full of messages from Shannon, going from eight or ten a day to now just one or two. At the first sound of her voice, Caroline hit the erase button and moved on to the next.

Shannon's words had stunned her. She'd expected any explanation other than the one she got and she was still shell shocked. Shannon loved her? Was *in love* with her? After all this time? So much had happened between them, to them, and with other women. How could she be? She was a totally different person than the spineless teenager who almost blindly followed her father's instructions. She was a grown woman, with different thoughts, beliefs, and goals in life. Or was she?

On their second night here, Fran had finally pried out of her exactly what had happened between them. As a good friend should, she let Caroline vent, spew, cuss, and cry before putting in her two cents' worth. Fran had admitted she had no idea what to say or do so she simply tried to keep her busy and had also acted as a lookout.

But now as they readied themselves at the starting line, Caroline knew Shannon was behind her. She didn't turn around to confirm her suspicion but could feel her gaze in the pinpricks on her back. She didn't know what to say to her. Shannon had declared her love and Caroline had casually walked away. She had thought about Shannon constantly since that afternoon and still had no clue what to do, where Shannon fit in her life. Or even if she did at all. But she did know what she needed to do today, right now. She needed to win this race. She had a game plan and she needed to stick to it. Shannon would only be a distraction to her wining the championship. I will not let that happen, she repeated to herself.

She checked her gear one last time. She had an extra bike tube in her pack along with a tire pump and four energy bars, and her CamelBak was full to the brim with the energy drink she needed to fuel her body. In the fanny pack strapped under her seat she stowed her repair kit, her bike wrenches, tube extractor, and the pocket knife she never left home without. In the pocket of her bike jersey was a pack of bubble gum and a tube of sunscreen ChapStick. Her face, arms, and the back of her neck were coated with SPF 50 sunscreen.

The race organizers intentionally started the race in the late afternoon. The excitement of the beginning and end of the race necessitated daylight hours. The riders usually made it through the darkness with minimal mishaps, but it was when dawn broke the next day that fatigue and lapses in concentration set in, resulting in falls, crashes, and flaring tempers.

It was 3:59 p.m. and Caroline was ready. She adjusted the fit of her gloves, the fit of her helmet on her head, and the snugness of her Oakley sunglasses protecting her eyes. The clock ticked down; thirty seconds to go. Caroline said a quick prayer. "God, give me strength and watch over all the riders today." She took several deep breaths, and as the starting horn sounded, the final race of her career began.

❖

Shannon was breathing much too hard and she knew it. She tried alternating her pace, slowing down, shifting gears. But she was still breathing too fast for this early in the race. The first three hours had been filled with jockeying for position around other slower, less experienced riders. Except for the burning in her lungs, she had settled into a comfortable rhythm, completing lap after lap without incident.

She glanced at her odometer secured just to the right of her left handlebar grip. She was struggling. Something was not right. Her gear was correct, her bike in top condition, but there was something wrong with her. Ever since she spilled her guts to Caroline, who had walked away without saying anything, she had felt like her world was collapsing around her. She couldn't keep any food down and battled waves of dizziness. It was as if her body was in shock.

Shannon expected the years of training to take over once the race began, shutting out everything except the feel of the course under her saddle. But for the first time in her racing career, it didn't. When the horn sounded, she hadn't overexerted to get ahead of the pack. She was a seasoned enough racer not to get caught up in the adrenaline of the start of the race and burn herself out too soon. She had laid back, assumed the pace she needed to take. The trail was marked in half-mile increments and she knew the pace she wanted to achieve for maximum results. It was a long twenty-four hours, and pace and tempo were important. So far, she was on track, if not slightly behind. If she found herself ahead, that would account for some of the fatigue she was feeling, but that wasn't the case. Rising out of her saddle gave her legs the extra push they needed to traverse a particularly nasty steep stretch of trail. She maneuvered around a rider repairing a flat tire and crested the trail. She barely noticed the breathtaking view of the Australian countryside before downshifting for the descent.

Shannon reached into the pocket in the back of her bike jersey and pulled out an energy bar. She used her teeth to rip off the end of the wrapper, then squeezed the coffee-colored bar out of the paper like a Popsicle out if its protective wrapper. She was careful to take only a small bite. She chewed it thoroughly and washed it down with her sport drink in the bottle cage between her legs. Again and again, she repeated the maneuver until she finished her energy bar and one complete bottle of her drink. She hoped she was able to keep it down.

After a sharp right hand turn, Shannon emerged onto a flat, dirt-packed road most people would consider a fire road. No wider than ten feet, it was used for fire suppression crews to get their machinery to the point of a fire as quickly as possible. It was on these roads that Shannon had first learned how to mountain bike and it was on these roads that Shannon had ridden the week before the championship series began. The roughness of the road, the dirt kicking up between her legs, the grit layering over her face, her eyes, and in her mouth was comforting. It was what she knew. It was what she was and she struggled to find her groove.

Squinting against the setting sun, Shannon saw Caroline fifty yards ahead. She had kept an eye on her lap after lap, stopping and resting when she did. Faster and faster she pedaled, and within minutes she was inches behind her. Five more strokes of her strong legs brought Shannon directly beside her.

"I have to talk to you," Shannon said between gulps of air. Caroline turned her head and by the shocked look on her face had not expected a conversation from anyone, let alone her main competitor.

"Are you out of your mind?" Caroline pedaled faster and Shannon easily caught up.

"I must be." She thought she had convinced herself not to approach Caroline. Her pride could only handle so much and another rejection wasn't included. But here she was, in the middle of the final race in the world championship, trying to talk to her. Another indication she had it bad for Caroline.

"I am not having a conversation with you. Get the hell out of here. Get the fuck out of my life."

Shannon tried several more times to talk with Caroline, but each time was met with staunch silence. Finally deciding their conversation would have to wait, she let up on the pedals and let Caroline slowly extend her lead.

❖

"Bike left." Caroline shouted the universal notification to riders ahead that there was a faster rider approaching. The line of riders stretched out in front of her for at least a mile, a cluster here, a group there, a single rider once in a while, but more often than not, at clusters of riders taking advantage of the drafting effect provided by the rider ahead of them. She hadn't seen Shannon since she tried to talk to her over an hour ago.

She passed a rider on a red Trek, downshifted, and increased her pace. She was twenty yards behind another woman in a bright yellow riding jersey and a hot pink helmet and as they approached a tight left turn, Caroline watched as if in slow motion. The rider's back tire lost traction and spun out from under her. She went down hard on the dirt. Caroline was far enough behind not to get caught up in the crash and asked, "You okay?" as she passed.

"Fuck yeah," came the reply. If the rider had been injured Caroline would have flagged down one of the race officials at the next mile marker.

She made it through the turn followed by another series of left and right turns, all the while pedaling faster and faster. She had to get away from Shannon. She hadn't been surprised when she pulled up beside her, but was absolutely stunned when Shannon started talking. Did she really expect her to carry on a conversation while in the middle of a race? What did she imagine she'd say? That she loved her too? Hell, up until a few days ago she didn't even like her, let alone love her. She certainly wasn't going to try to figure it out in the middle of the most important race in her career. Was it a ploy to make her lose concentration so she could have some advantage over her? Who knew, and frankly, Caroline told herself, she didn't care. She couldn't care, at least not right now. She had a race to win.

Her legs pushed and pulled against the pedals, the memory of the thousands of hours of training that led up to this point making them work. She released her grip on the handlebar, grabbed the tube of her CamelBak and stuck it between her teeth all in one smooth motion. She took a couple of short sips making sure she didn't choke on the cool liquid, giving her body the chance to absorb the much needed nutrients.

Passing a few riders struggling to climb the steep trail, Caroline's lungs burned and her legs ached. But she wasn't worried about it. She had planned her race in just this manner and so far, everything was going as planned. Downshifting into third gear, Caroline completed the ascent over sharp rocks and obstacles. The trail leveled off and she downshifted, increasing her speed and continuing to maintain control of her bike. She'd been riding for three hours and twenty-nine minutes and she knew she was near the end of the lap.

The road was rough. Her legs and arms acted like shock absorbers getting a complete and thorough workout. It was for this reason she pushed herself so hard in the gym, almost to the point of exhaustion. At this critical point, she had the stamina and her muscles the strength to continue.

She had spent months with her trainer Carlos, lifting, sweating, and running, all the while hating him with one breath and thanking him with the next. The mental toughness was something no one could train her in except herself. Other riders meditated or hired therapists to help them achieve the mental toughness they needed. Caroline simply listened to her body.

Prior to each race, she memorized the course so that she knew exactly where every turn, dip, and obstacle was and planned her attack accordingly. When her hard work and training were in sync, she rode her best race. Sometimes she was not the winner or even second or third, but her time was respectable and most importantly she had read her body and the course perfectly. And that's what she was striving for.

The riders were on their own during the race. Other than medical services, they could not receive any help or assistance. Any repairs needed had to be completed by the rider only and no coaching was allowed. For the entire twenty-four hours it was a test of mental toughness. Mind over matter when your brain was screaming to your body to slow down, shut down, to stop. It was mental toughness and tenacity that would win this race. Caroline had it, and she knew it.

Night fell as Caroline pulled into her rest area. Based on her race plan, this was the time she had scheduled to take a break, rehydrate, and refuel. As she nibbled on an energy bar she snapped her light in the bracket on her handlebars and one on her helmet. The NiteRider would illuminate the ground in front of her for about twenty yards, giving her enough time to adjust her line as darkness closed in. Her night gear in place, Caroline lay on her back, elevating her legs. Her feet were swollen and her back hurt from the hours of constant beating. Her plan to rest and refuel for thirty minutes was scuttled by a familiar voice above her head.

"Caroline." Shannon's voice pleaded.

"Go away. I have nothing to say to you. Especially now." Caroline hadn't expected Shannon to follow her into her tent. The shadow from the small lantern made Shannon appear larger than she was. Shannon didn't move.

"How else do I have to say it to you, Shannon? I don't want you in my life. You are not good for me. You are not the kind of woman I need even if I wanted you. And I don't. We hooked up again and it was like old times, but that's all it was. A mutual thing. Now leave me alone." Caroline practically shouted in frustration. She was trying to win the biggest race of her career and she was having a lovers' quarrel instead. She grabbed her helmet and pulled her bike through the small opening and into the night.

"Fuck!" Caroline shouted into the darkness. She hadn't had

enough rest and when she hit the dirt after missing the turn she was tempted to lie there. Repeating the curse, she checked to make sure she wasn't seriously injured and slowly got to her feet. Using the light on her helmet, she surveyed the condition of her bike. The only damage appeared to be a slight tear on the edge of her seat and she remounted intending on finishing the lap.

How could she be so careless? She was thinking about Shannon and not paying attention to the road in front of her and look what it got her—a fresh batch of road rash on her leg, dirt down the front of her shirt, and thoroughly pissed off.

Lap after lap she rode, one hour melting into the other until finally, the sun began to creep over the horizon. She hadn't seen Shannon all night and had no idea if she was ahead of her in the lap count or not. At noon, the current standings would be posted and Caroline knew that's when the race really began.

CHAPTER TWENTY-TWO

Shannon was exhausted. Her legs felt like rubber, her eyes burned, there was a painful cramp in her right hand, and she had lost feeling in her ass hours ago. Forty minutes remained in the race and she was behind Caroline by half a lap. It wasn't an insurmountable lead, under any other circumstance, but this was anything but. She didn't think she had it in her to chase after Caroline, let alone catch her. She was physically drained and mentally numb. She was pedaling by rote, braking more often now than in the first forty minutes of the race. Her lips were chapped, dried blood snaked a path in the mud caked from knee to sock, and the gash at her elbow dripped blood onto her thigh. She was a mess and it was only by sheer guts that she was able to stay in the saddle.

She hadn't seen Caroline since just after two this morning and had stopped looking for her long before that. Caroline had made it painfully clear that she wanted nothing to do with her, and as much as it hurt, Shannon let her go. She wasn't going to chase after someone who didn't want to be caught. She had said her peace. The rest was up to Caroline.

❖

Don't fall, don't trip, don't stumble, the cadence in Caroline's head echoed with each step. Her head was spinning, her heart racing in direct competition with the shaking of her legs as she climbed to the top of the winner's platform. The crowd chanted her name as she finally arrived at her destination.

This was more than about winning, much, much more. It was the achievement of everything she had worked a lifetime for. Millions of beads of sweat, thousands of hours of practice, and untold sacrifices to get to this point. She was the best in the world. She had proven it. To herself, her critics, and her adversaries.

She was finally here. She should be euphoric, ecstatic, on top of the world. It should be the happiest day of her life. But all she felt was empty. Hundreds of people surrounded her, but she was alone, totally alone when it really mattered.

She scanned the crowd searching for the only person that mattered. She recognized many familiar faces, but none contained the crystal clear eyes that she desperately wanted to see. Sometime during the last hours of the race, when her body was exhausted, her mind unable to fight the fatigue, her heart had taken over.

She loved Shannon. It was that simple. It was so simple she couldn't even see it until her cluttered mind was empty. She heard Shannon's words in her head and very easily could repeat them word for word. She had been in love with Shannon in high school but had attributed it to a rite of passage everyone went through at that age. And as she had always thought, that love was supposed to be intense, fleeting, and as a result, painful. It had been all three but also all wrong. Her feelings for Shannon had been intense and painful, but Caroline realized they were not fleeting.

The way they had avoided each other for years, never sharing more than a few words when their two different racing tours coincided kept her feelings for Shannon buried. But they were just below the surface all along, and after that night, that wonderful night, could never be buried again. Her name was called and Caroline stepped forward.

After the pomp and circumstance of the awards ceremony, the interviews and countless pictures, Caroline was finally alone in her hotel room. Her medal hung heavy around her neck and it clunked loudly as she dropped it on the oak table. She grabbed a bottle of cold water from the minibar and kicked off her shoes. There was a knock on the door when the lid on the bottle cracked open. Her heart jumped and the first name that came to mind was Shannon. Having finished fourth, she didn't need to be at the awards ceremony and she wasn't. Other than their discussion in her tent last night, Caroline had successfully avoided Shannon for most of the week. She prayed her luck had not run out. She still had no idea what to do with her feelings for Shannon going forward.

Looking through the peephole, Caroline sighed, unlocked, and opened the door. "Hey," was her greeting as Fran walked into the room.

"Hey yourself. Where'd you run off to? We looked for you at the party. Your parents sent me on the search mission." She hesitated. "You okay?"

Caroline didn't want to get into it with Fran. She was physically tired, emotionally exhausted, and for one frightening moment she thought she was going to cry. She'd made her views known, told Shannon to leave her alone, never speak to her again. How could she go back to her now? She was going to cry over Shannon Roberts. Been there, done that, and she was going to do it again and again.

"Yeah, fine. Just a little tired." Caroline busied herself with opening her bottle of water. She offered one to Fran who shook her head as she plopped in the chair by the small desk. She knew Fran well enough to read her body language and Fran had just settled in for a long, probing interrogation.

"Come on, Caroline."

Caroline crossed the room and pulled the curtains to shut out the setting sun. She took a long moment before turning and facing Fran.

"There is nothing to talk about. We got together for old time's sake. She moved on and so have I." It was a rather succinct explanation. It was the truth. At least the first two parts. She was going to have to work on the third.

"And?" Fran wasn't going to accept her explanation at face value.

"And nothing. It happened, and it won't happen again." Caroline didn't know if she was trying to convince Fran or herself. She kept talking to do both. "I don't fit in her life and she definitely doesn't fit in mine."

"What does that mean?"

"Come on, Fran, you know what I'm talking about. We haven't

said more than three things to each other in ten years. Other than riding her bike and sleeping with more women than I even know, I have no idea what she does with her life. And it doesn't matter. It was just a trip down memory lane. Nothing more, nothing less."

"You are so full of shit. How do you even stand yourself?" Fran hadn't moved or even raised her voice. "Don't bullshit a bullshitter. I've seen the way you can't keep your eyes off her. You knew every minute of every day where Shannon was this week. And you wanted to be with her. Just admit it and stop pretending she doesn't still mean something to you."

"Shut up, Fran," Caroline said louder than she intended. "Just shut up. You have no idea what I want and certainly not what I'm thinking. The season is over. I've done what I wanted to do. I won the championship. I'm the best rider in the world. Now it's time to grow up and be a big girl. In three weeks, I'll be standing in front of six people who will judge me like I have never been judged before. They will control whether or not I get to do what I've always dreamed of. Those men will have my future in the palms of their pompous, fat, little hands. I don't need any more pressure right now and I certainly don't need any more shit about Shannon Roberts, so please just shut the fuck up."

CHAPTER TWENTY-THREE

Shannon smoothed the nonexistent wrinkles out of her pants and centered the gleaming silver buckle on her belt. She was more nervous than she expected to be. She still wasn't sure why she was here. She had nothing in common with these people except for the fact that they had gone to the same school ten years ago. She hadn't spoken to any of them since the day Caroline's father walked into Caroline's room and changed Shannon's life forever. If not for the pictures in Facebook, she probably wouldn't recognize any of the people here if they walked past her on the street. It still wasn't too late to turn around and leave. And do what? Go back to her empty hotel room and drink? Worse yet, think, remember? She'd been doing enough of that lately, especially the drinking part. Whoever said drinking washed away sadness never had her heart broken by Caroline Davis.

The tastefully ornate sign indicated the Grand Ballroom was to her left. The lobby of the Marriott Royale Resort was as stuffy and pretentious as she remembered from the time she and her parents stayed there when they had come to visit the campus of Mount Holyfield. Good God, was it almost fifteen years ago when they had spent the weekend touring and interviewing with the administration and faculty? For a moment Shannon wondered if Dean Phillips would be in attendance. What would she say to her now?

Subdued music led her to the large room decorated with balloons—green and white, the school colors of MHA. A large sign that read WELCOME ALUMNI hung over the wide double doors. People floated in and out of the room chatting and laughing, many of them holding champagne glasses.

Shannon hung back observing the scene. The women were immaculately dressed in an assortment of cocktail dresses and evening wear. They were all thin, almost to the point of being emaciated, and made up to the point of being comical. More than one pair of surgically enhanced breasts passed in front of her.

The men were equally stylish. Some had donned tuxedos for the event, others simply wore dark suits with conservative power ties. They were as tan as if they had just stepped off the tennis court or a week on a yacht. The people and the place reeked of old money, superficial smiles, and air kisses. And what in the hell was she doing in the middle of it? She had absolutely no idea but kept putting one foot in front of the other.

Unclenching her fists, Shannon walked to the registration table. Three women way too perky to be for real greeted her. "Hello, welcome to our reunion. Your name?" The women looked at her, searching her face for anything that would jog their memories for Shannon's name. Shannon knew there were many memories. She was the proverbial bad girl and she was certain her last week at MHA had become a legend.

"Shannon Roberts." Shannon watched as the woman with hair too dark to be natural recognized her name. She looked her up and down as if searching for any sign that the scandal that had forced her out of Mount Holyfield was still clinging to her. The other woman squinted as if she couldn't see Shannon clearly without the glasses she probably refused to wear.

"Here you are. Shannon Roberts. My, you haven't changed a bit," she said looking between Shannon and the picture on her name tag. She finally handed it to her.

"Thanks." Shannon glanced at the picture and cringed. God, she hoped she didn't still look like that.

"We're in the room to the right. Dinner is at seven, the program starts at eight, and dancing after that. Did you bring a guest?"

Shannon barely recognized there was a question in the high-pitched chatter from the woman. "No," she replied and stepped toward the door to her past.

Ten years, she repeated to herself. She hadn't given MHA anything more than a passing thought since the day she left. Now she was expected to mix and mingle with women she had barely spoken with in high school and make inane small talk with their husbands. She seriously doubted that any of the other lesbians at MHA would be in attendance with their girlfriends. But then again neither was she.

Snagging a glass of champagne from a passing waiter, Shannon stepped further into the crowded room. Several heads turned her way and she vaguely recognized a few faces. But they knew who she was. The expressions on their faces told her as much. After the incident with Caroline's father, a few of her friends had managed to get in touch with her. Her absence hadn't gone unnoticed and she was the subject of just about every conversation on campus. Rumors were rampant. She had heard they included everything from stories that she ran off with a college coed from Tufts University in Boston to suggestions that she was pregnant. Shannon had had a good laugh over that one.

Shannon expected this when she had RSVP'd to the reunion committee chairman that she would be attending. She had checked the box, licked the envelope, and dropped it in the corner mailbox the week after she'd returned from Australia. In the weeks since, she had hashed and rehashed her decision and at the last minute almost didn't come. She was getting dressed when a case of second thoughts crashed in on her. Why was she going? Did she have something to prove? To whom? Herself? Dean Phillips? The other members of her senior class? She was a graduate just like they were, even if she didn't walk down the aisle to the tune of "Pomp and Circumstance." She deserved to be here.

Shannon had asked herself those questions plus a few hundred more in the days leading up to tonight. She was no closer to an answer now that she was here than when she was sitting on her deck last week in Big Bear. She was as much alone then as she was right now.

Before she had a chance to contemplate her state of mind any further she was grabbed from behind and spun around and ended up face-to-face with Marci McMillan. Marci with an *i*, as she always said when she introduced herself, was at least thirty pounds lighter and had much larger breasts than the last time Shannon had seen her.

"Oh my God, Shannon!" she exclaimed causing several people to look their way. "Is it really you?"

"Marci, how are you? You look great," Shannon managed to say when her ex-roommate finally turned her loose.

"I'm fine, and thanks. After three trips to the fat farm, I finally got it right. Bernard promised me if I lost the weight and kept it off for two years he'd buy me a new pair of boobs." It was obvious that Marci had accomplished her long-term weight loss and was proud of it.

"Very nice."

"Shannon, you look great too. What's your secret?" Marci asked in a co-conspirator tone.

"Nothing as exciting as you, Marci." Shannon knew she looked like hell. She wasn't sleeping, the circles under her eyes were darker on her now pale skin. She had lost weight, her naturally lean body was painfully thin. A glass of Chivas more often than not was her evening meal. When she first returned from Australia it was her lunch and sometimes her breakfast as well. She looked for the passing tray of alcohol. Marci grabbed her arm and practically dragged her across the room. Marci's voice was far more animated than Shannon remembered.

"You have got to come see Beth and Courtney. They are going to crap when they see you."

Approaching the women in question, Shannon steeled herself to face two of the biggest snobby, self-righteous, bigoted, girly girls at MHA. One look at them and Shannon knew they had only refined those traits as the years passed.

"Girls, look who's here! Shannon Roberts. We were just talking about whether or not she'd be here tonight and I looked up and there she was. Can you believe it?"

Taking the high road, Shannon held out her hand first to Beth Hardel. "Hello, Beth." Beth took one look at her outstretched hand, then back to Shannon. She saw the look of disapproval Beth didn't even bother to hide as she passed judgment on Shannon's choice of wardrobe for the evening. More out of politeness and good breeding, Beth finally took her hand. Shannon repeated the same greeting to Courtney.

Marci filled the awkward silence. "Shannon, what are you doing with yourself? I didn't see your profile on Facebook." The reunion committee had encouraged all alumni to create a Facebook page so that they all could reconnect even if they weren't able to attend the event.

"I didn't know until the last minute I was coming. What about you, Marci?" Shannon switched the topic without answering the question posed to her.

Shannon listened with half an ear to Marci drone on about her husband and kids and when the talk between the women turned to the trials of braces and puberty, she tuned out all but the essentials and merely nodded when she thought it appropriate. Her name brought her attention back to the women in front of her.

"I'm sorry, what did you say?" She hadn't heard whether she was asked a question or simply was supposed to respond to a statement.

"I asked if you were married or had any children?" Beth said too sweetly.

Shannon knew Beth was intentionally trying to embarrass her with the question. Beth had hated her in high school and obviously still did. She thought Shannon unworthy of a school like Mount Holyfield and had told her so on more than one occasion.

"No, I'm not. They don't allow lesbians to get married in the state I live in." Shannon let the statement hang in the air. She had nothing to hide, especially from these people. She didn't care what they thought. Never had and never would. That same apathy clouded her judgment more and more every day. She knew she was depressed, but like everything else lately she didn't seem to have the energy to face it, let alone tackle it. With a wicked sense of perverted pleasure, she watched the color drain from Beth's perfectly made up face to be replaced by an unattractive shade of green disgust. Shannon continued looking her straight in the eye while she waited for what would come next.

"That's disgusting. You're disgusting, Shannon Roberts. I always knew you were a pervert. You were always looking at me that way." Beth emphasized her last two words.

"Actually, Beth, I never gave you a second thought. I prefer my lovers to be passionate and alive. You never did fit the bill. Still don't, I see. If you ladies will excuse me." Shannon left all three women standing with their mouths open, one laughing, the other two speechless.

A prickling along the back of her neck made her pause. It was the same feeling she always got just before she caught Caroline staring at her. Her heart beat against her chest and she suddenly felt lightheaded. She maneuvered around several couples laughing loudly and past the buffet table. She knew that unless she left now, she wouldn't be able to avoid Caroline all night. She didn't think Caroline would come. She had said as much at the race and when Shannon couldn't help herself and had Googled Caroline last week, a press release from NASA stated that she had accepted a position and would immediately be entering the astronaut training program.

What would she see when she turned around? More precisely, who would she see with Caroline? It had been a little more than two months since she had seen her in Australia and Caroline had been celebrating with Fran. That was one of many images that kept her awake at night. Finally ready to face Caroline and whoever she brought with her, Shannon turned around.

It was about goddamned time, Caroline thought. She had been nervously following Shannon around the ballroom for fifteen minutes before she turned her way. She was stunning in her faux tuxedo, deep red shirt, and shiny black loafers. Her hair was a little longer, but not much. She looked tired and thinner but still wore that same cloak of edgy confidence and looked totally at ease in this crowd.

She had scoured the room when she first arrived for any sign of Shannon. Even though her name was on the list of attendees, Caroline didn't know if Shannon would actually be there. She had tried and failed miserably during the past week not to get her hopes up lest she be disappointed.

Caroline knew there was music playing but didn't hear anything except the drumming of her heart and the pounding in her ears. When their eyes met, her stomach flipped several times and her hand shook so bad she almost spilled her cocktail. It was that same look. The same intense gaze as if Shannon could see right through her and into her soul and know what she was thinking. If that were true, Shannon would know that Caroline had thought about her often in the last few weeks. She had relived their one night together in Austria more times than she could count, remembering and savoring each taste and touch of her. She had shed a million tears in the last two months over losing her again. Especially after realizing she was hopelessly in love with her.

She approached Shannon and watched the expression on her face. There was a spark of joy that was quickly covered up with steely reserve. Caroline wet her lips nervously as she closed the distance between them.

"Hello, Shannon. It's good to see you." Caroline was surprised that her voice sounded normal. She was outwardly calm and restrained but what she really wanted to do was throw herself in Shannon's arms and never let go. Her heart threatened to stop when Shannon didn't immediately reply.

"You too. I didn't know you'd be here. I didn't expect a renowned astrophysicist, soon-to-be-astronaut, would come to a small town class reunion."

Caroline's chuckle came out sounding more like a strangled cry. "Hardly. I just got my Ph.D. and I haven't even started work yet." The fact that she had postponed her start date with NASA she kept to herself. Somehow she had made it through defending her dissertation, and just barely at that. She was an emotional mess and knew that if she didn't get her shit together before starting at NASA she would fail and fail miserably.

"Maybe I wanted everyone to see what a swanky private school can produce?" Caroline continued trying to lighten her mood. "Maybe I wanted to relive my youth?" Shannon laughed. Caroline jumped off the cliff of her emotions. Her love for Shannon gave her the strength to take the first step. "Maybe I just wanted to see you."

Caroline said it so quietly and calmly it caught her off guard. She knew what she wanted to say to Shannon, had practiced it dozens of times, but she hadn't expected to say it within the first three minutes. Her world was spinning, and she was being carried along for the ride. "I'm sorry. That didn't come out quite as I had planned." Her heart jumped back in her throat and for a moment she thought she might be sick. "Can we go somewhere and talk?" Caroline glanced around at the noisy crowd. She heard the faint pleading in her voice. She desperately wanted to talk to Shannon. No she needed to talk to her. To explain, to ask for another chance, to beg if she had to.

Shannon lowered her eyes and shifted her weight from one foot to the other. Then she looked at Caroline as if deciding if she would say yes or no. Caroline got very nervous.

"Sure, how about outside? There's a nice patio across the courtyard." Shannon motioned in the direction of the exit doors.

Caroline led the way feeling Shannon's eyes on her bare back. She had chosen her dress carefully for just this occasion. She was the opposite of her techno-geek degree and was bound and determined to look perfect if she was lucky enough to see Shannon again. Fran had the fashion sense Caroline lacked and the checkbook to pay for a designer label and had gone with her to pick out the Kate Spade dress.

The deep plum color of the dress complemented her dark hair and complexion and more than half the men in the room had looked twice when she entered. The high neckline gave no indication of the plunging back that tapered to a straight skirt that hung just above her knees. Black sheer stockings and matching pumps completed her outfit. Her hair was up in a French braid, accentuating her bare shoulders. Her jewelry was a simple silver watch and diamond stud earrings. She had barely recognized herself when she looked in the mirror.

Shannon had to remember to put one foot in front of the other as she followed Caroline out of the room and across the atrium to the patio. She was stunned by Caroline's admission that she wanted to see her. She had as much as told her to drop dead months ago. Whatever could she want to say to her now?

Caroline was the most beautiful woman she had ever seen. She was sophisticated, lovely, and every degree a very successful woman. It took everything she had to wait for Caroline to speak.

"Are you still riding?"

Shannon chuckled. She hadn't been on a bike since the finals. "Not much. I own a bike shop in Big Bear, California. It's just a small place. You know, a few bikes, some gear, that sort of thing. It doubles as a ski shop in the winter." Shannon had bought the shop several years earlier as an investment and had barely stepped foot in it. Until recently. She had taken to spending more and more time in it trying to occupy her mind from persistent thoughts of Caroline.

"Sounds perfect for you."

"Yeah, well a girl's gotta do something to make a living."

Good God, Caroline thought. We're standing here talking as if we were long lost lovers who've just run into each other on the street. They were anything but, and she was not about to tiptoe around it again. "I've missed you." Caroline's declaration came out of nowhere and she was not prepared for its powerful simplicity.

"Caroline—"

"Shannon, please, let me talk." Caroline stepped closer, Shannon's familiar scent drifting in the air. "You were the best thing that ever happened in my life. You were when we were seventeen and you were again during the championship."

"And you came all this way just to tell me that?"

Caroline bit back the pain at the sarcasm in Shannon's voice. It wasn't much but it was there nonetheless. It hurt but she knew she deserved it. She closed the distance between them. Her hands trembled as she took Shannon's.

"No, not really. I came because when Marci said that you were going to be here I couldn't help myself. I wanted to see you again. I *needed* to see you."

Caroline couldn't take her eyes off Shannon even if she wanted to—and she didn't. She never wanted Shannon out of her sight again, but Shannon's restraint and body language told her she didn't want the same. Her nerve fluttered and before she had a chance to change her mind she spoke again. "I was stupid. I didn't give you a chance. I didn't think we had anything special, anything that we could build a future on. All we did was dance around each other and when we stopped moving all we did was fight. I couldn't see what was right in front of me. I pushed you away." Caroline stopped and let her words sink in. "And I've regretted it ever since."

Shannon said nothing, her face betraying nothing as well. She couldn't give up, not when Shannon was this close. "I love you, Shannon. I loved you in high school and I love you now. I didn't know it ten years ago or even three months ago, but I know it now."

Caroline took Shannon's hands in hers. A shiver of familiarity melted through her body where the hard calluses had caressed her, worshiped her, brought her to orgasm time and time again, loved her. "I have nothing to lose because if I don't have you then I don't have anything. You're in my heart, under my skin, in every breath I take. I need you in my life. You make my life complete. You make me happy, you make me angry, and you make me feel loved." Caroline took a half step back so she could look directly into Shannon's eyes. Caroline could feel the heat coming off Shannon's body, smell her, taste her lips. She sensed Shannon's emotions were barely in check and took advantage of the situation. "I love you and I want to build a life with you. If you'll have me." It wouldn't be easy. They lived in different places, had careers they were devoted to. But they'd figure it out.

Shannon was not prepared for Caroline's declaration and it felt as if the rug had been pulled out from under her again. Her stomach was somewhere in the vicinity of her throat battling for position with her hammering heart. She had wanted exactly this. In Australia she had declared her love and wanted Caroline to say exactly what she just did. But she tossed her aside like yesterday's newspaper and Shannon had been devastated. She couldn't go through that again. Hell, she was nowhere near through it now. What if Caroline changed her mind again? What if they couldn't agree on anything and it didn't work? What if it did?

Suddenly her mind shut down and she was looking into the eyes of the most beautiful woman in the world. The woman who had taken her heart when she least expected it was looking at her, waiting for her answer. It was her decision and hers alone that would shape the rest of their lives. Caroline's hands held hers tightly giving her the strength she never thought she needed. There was only one answer. She leaned in and whispered, "I love you too, Caroline." Then she kissed her.

About the Author

Julie Cannon is a corporate stiff by day and dreamer by night. She has six other books published by Bold Strokes Books: *Come and Get Me*, *Heart 2 Heart*, *Heartland*, *Uncharted Passage*, *Just Business*, and *Power Play*. Julie has also published four short stories in Bold Strokes anthologies. A recent transplant to Houston, Julie and her partner Laura live on a lake with their two kids, two dogs, and a cat.

Visit Julie at www.juliecannon.com.

Books Available From Bold Strokes Books

The Devil be Damned by Ali Vali. The fourth book in the best-selling Cain Casey Devil series. (978-1-60282-159-0)

Descent by Julie Cannon. Shannon Roberts and Caroline Davis compete in the world of world-class bike racing and pretend that the fire between them is just professional rivalry, not desire. (978-1-60282-160-6)

Kiss of Noir by Clara Nipper. Nora Delany is a hard-living, sweet-talking woman who can't say no to a beautiful babe or a friend in danger—a darkly humorous homage to a bygone era of tough broads and murder in steamy New Orleans. (978-1-60282-161-3)

Under Her Skin by Lea Santos. Supermodel Lilly Lujan hasn't a care in the world, except life is lonely in the spotlight—until Mexican gardener Torien Pacias sees through Lilly's facade and offers gentle understanding and friendship when Lilly most needs it. (978-1-60282-162-0)

Fierce Overture by Gun Brooke. Helena Forsythe is a hard-hitting CEO who gets what she wants by taking no prisoners when negotiating—until she meets a woman who convinces her that charm may be the way to win a battle, and a heart. (978-1-60282-156-9)

Trauma Alert by Radclyffe. Dr. Ali Torveau has no trouble saying no to romance until the day firefighter Beau Cross shows up in her ER and sets her carefully ordered world aflame. (978-1-60282-157-6)

Wolfsbane Winter by Jane Fletcher. Iron Wolf mercenary Deryn faces down demon magic and otherworldly foes with a smile, but she's defenseless when healer Alana wages war on her heart. (978-1-60282-158-3)

Little White Lie by Lea Santos. Emie Jaramillo knows relationships are for other people, and beautiful women like Gia Mendez don't belong anywhere near her boring world of academia—until Gia sets out to convince Emie she has not only brains, but beauty…and that she's the only woman Gia wants in her life. (978-1-60282-163-7)

Witch Wolf by Winter Pennington. In a world where vampires have charmed their way into modern society, where werewolves walk the streets with their beasts disguised by human skin, Investigator Kassandra Lyall has a secret of her own to protect. She's one of them. (978-1-60282-177-4)

Do Not Disturb by Carsen Taite. Ainsley Faraday, a high-powered executive, and rock music celebrity Greer Davis couldn't be less well suited for one another, and yet they soon discover passion has a way of designing its own future. (978-1-60282-153-8)

From This Moment On by PJ Trebelhorn. Devon Conway and Katherine Hunter both lost love and neither believes they will ever find it again—until the moment they meet and everything changes. (978-1-60282-154-5)

Vapor by Larkin Rose. When erotic romance writer Ashley Vaughn decides to take her research into the bedroom for a night of passion with Victoria Hadley, she discovers that fact is hotter than fiction. (978-1-60282-155-2)

Wind and Bones by Kristin Marra. Jill O'Hara, award-winning journalist, just wants to settle her deceased father's affairs and leave Prairie View, Montana, far, far behind—but an old girlfriend, a sexy sheriff, and a dangerous secret keep her down on the ranch. (978-1-60282-150-7)

Nightshade by Shea Godfrey. The story of a princess, betrothed as a political pawn, who falls for her intended husband's soldier sister, is a modern-day fairy tale to capture the heart. (978-1-60282-151-4)

Vieux Carré Voodoo by Greg Herren. Popular New Orleans detective Scotty Bradley just can't stay out of trouble—especially when an old flame turns up asking for help. (978-1-60282-152-1)

The Pleasure Set by Lisa Girolami. Laney DeGraff, a successful president of a family-owned bank on Rodeo Drive, finds her comfortable life taking a turn toward danger when Theresa Aguilar, a sleek, sexy lawyer, invites her to join an exclusive, secret group of powerful, alluring women. (978-1-60282-144-6)

A Perfect Match by Erin Dutton. The exciting world of pro golf forms the backdrop for a fast-paced, sexy romance. (978-1-60282-145-3)

Father Knows Best by Lynda Sandoval. High school juniors and best friends Lila Moreno, Meryl Morganstern, and Caressa Thibodoux plan to make the most of the summer before senior year. What they discover that amazing summer about girl power, growing up, and trusting friends and family more than prepares them to tackle that all-important senior year! (978-1-60282-147-7)

The Midnight Hunt by L.L. Raand. Medic Drake McKennan takes a chance and loses, and her life will never be the same—because when she wakes up after surviving a life-threatening illness, she is no longer human. (978-1-60282-140-8)

Long Shot by D. Jackson Leigh. Love isn't safe, which is exactly why equine veterinarian Tory Greyson wants no part of it—until Leah Montgomery and a horse that won't give up convince her otherwise. (978-1-60282-141-5)

In Medias Res by Yolanda Wallace. Sydney has forgotten her entire life, and the one woman who holds the key to her memory, and her heart, doesn't want to be found. (978-1-60282-142-2)

Awakening to Sunlight by Lindsey Stone. Neither Judith or Lizzy is looking for companionship, and certainly not love—but when their lives become entangled, they discover both. (978-1-60282-143-9)

Fever by VK Powell. Hired gun Zakaria Chambers is hired to provide a simple escort service to philanthropist Sara Ambrosini, but nothing is as simple as it seems, especially love. (978-1-60282-135-4)

Truths by Rebecca S. Buck. Two women separated by two hundred years are connected by fate and love. (978-1-60282-146-0)

High Risk by JLee Meyer. Can actress Kate Hoffman really risk all she's worked for to take a chance on love? Or is it already too late? (978-1-60282-136-1)

Spanking New by Clifford Henderson. A poignant, hilarious, unforgettable look at life, love, gender, and the essence of what makes us who we are. (978-1-60282-138-5)

Missing Lynx by Kim Baldwin and Xenia Alexiou. On the trail of a notorious serial killer, Elite Operative Lynx's growing attraction to a mysterious mercenary could be her path to love—or to death. (978-1-60282-137-8)

Magic of the Heart by C.J. Harte. CEO Susan Hettinger and wild, impulsive rock star M.J. Carson couldn't be more different if they tried—but opposites attract in ways neither woman can resist. (978-1-60282-131-6)

Ambereye by Gill McKnight. Jolie Garoul is falling in love with her assistant. The big problem is, Jolie is a werewolf. (978-1-60282-132-3)

Collision Course by C.P. Rowlands. Tragedy leaves Brie O'Malley and Jordan Carter fearful and alone. Can they find the courage to take a second chance on love? (978-1-60282-133-0)

Mephisto Aria by Justine Saracen. Opera singer Katherina Marov's destiny may be to repeat the mistakes of her father when she becomes involved in a dangerous love affair. (978-1-60282-134-7)

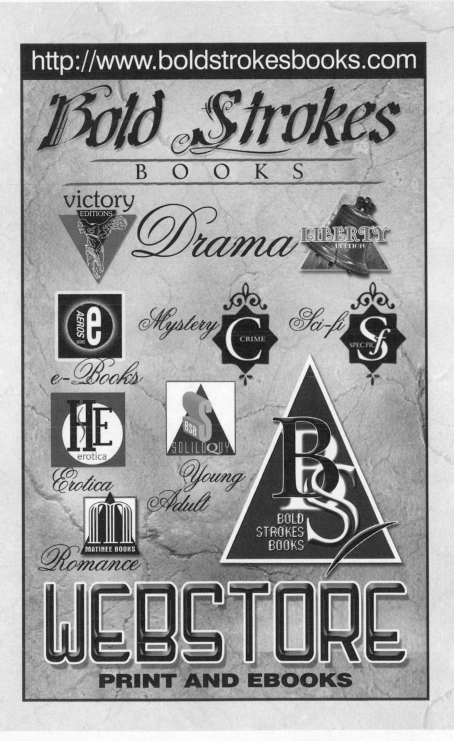